ROCKY POINT HERO

Rocky Point Series, Book Four

BARBARA MCMAHON

Rocky Point Hero
Copyright © 2013 Barbara McMahon
All Rights Reserved

Chapter One

Allie Turner settled in to wait, braced in the crevasse, the rocks on either side steadying her arms. The surface was cold, uneven and uncomfortable. She'd risked a fall scrambling down the cliff in the dark with only a flashlight, but the timing had to be perfect. She shivered as the sea swirled below her, imagining some of the spray drifted up in the breezy predawn sky. It was cold enough without any more dampness to add to the chill.

Slowly the sky lightened. The stars faded first, and the darkness was gradually replaced by daylight. She could almost feel the sun about to rise above the horizon. She took aim. Waited. Patience, she thought, feeling her leg going to sleep. This was her third try. She wanted to make sure it was her last. Getting up in the dark, picking her way down the rocky cliff wasn't something she made a habit of. Today was the day; she just knew it.

Peering at the horizon, she hoped she timed it right: the first rays were beginning to shoot over. Slowly her finger pressed the trigger, shot after shot as the sky lightened, hoping for the illusive green flash. There. The camera took another picture, another, and another. She'd fill her entire card if she had to. Slowly the sun began rising as if from the dark sea itself. She quickly swapped a filter and began shooting again. The sea was like glass in the distance, reflecting the rising orb perfectly as it began the day.

At last she lowered the camera, a feeling of satisfaction sweeping through her. She couldn't wait to see the picture and make sure she'd captured the exact images she hoped for. It would be a spectacular finish to the annual report for SeaRovers Inc. Optimistic, forward thinking. The dawning of the new year for a growing company. Just the images they wanted to project.

Stiff from sitting on the hard granite, she slowly eased around, trying to get comfortable as she returned her lenses and camera to the sturdy case, slipping the flashlight inside as well. Slipping the bag over her shoulder, she stretched out her leg and shook her foot, getting pins and needles for her efforts. With a grimace she rose to her feet, found her balance and looked up toward the top of the cliff thirty feet away. Taking a breath against the familiar pain in her hip, she began climbing back to the top. It was easier on the way up, with the light to help her find her way.

Cresting the rim a few moments later, she breathed a sigh of relief. She'd done that descent several times but the danger still scared her. A wrong step and she could end up smashed at the bottom, washed away to sea, never found again. She shivered. Her parents would be horrified to know what she was doing. Which is why she rarely talked about the ways she obtained some of her photographs.

"Thank you, Lord, for being with me. And for giving me

the perfect picture. I hope at least one turns out perfect."

Looking around, she spotted her cane a few feet to the left. Scooping it up, she leaned on it for a moment, massaging her hip and thigh. She'd probably feel the ache all day with the strain of the climb. A smile lit her face, however. It'd been worth it.

Walking carefully across the weeds and grass on the uneven ground, she reached the end of the gravel road and turned to walk along the edge to her car. She wished for the firmness of asphalt, but that wasn't going to happen here at the end of Water Street. She just had to watch where she was walking. Which was hard when the morning was so fresh and clear, with not a cloud anywhere. She wanted to look around her, at the sea gradually turning a deep blue. At the town in the distance hugging the cove. It was going to be a beautiful Indian summer day.

As she approached the edge of the pavement, she glanced beyond her car at the last house on the old road. When she'd passed it earlier, there'd been lights on inside. Another early riser. Now she could just make out a man standing on the porch, cup in hand. He wasn't close enough for her to see clearly, but he appeared to be watching her. Probably wondering what in the world she was doing out at the crack of dawn.

She knew someone was staying at the Stafford house, as she'd seen lights on when she'd driven by on her way to the cliff the last couple of mornings. Usually tapped into the town's gossip mill, she hadn't heard it'd been rented. It wasn't an easy house to let. The dwelling itself had seen better days.

A large, two story wooden home, the wood siding was weathered and scoured clean of paint on the windward side. The yard was practically non-existent; the proximity to the salt from the sea air made grass almost impossible to grow. And with it being vacant for long stretches, no one kept up flowers or shrubs.

Still, it had been built over a hundred years ago. Sturdy and dependable, it had stood the test of time. Who had the Staffords' estate rented it to this time, she wondered? The summer season had ended at Labor Day. Pretty much the only people around now were the year-round residents.

Before she got into her SUV, she impulsively gave a wave.

The man appeared to hesitate, then lifted his cup in silent salute.

He looked tall. Beyond that she couldn't tell if he was young or old, with dark hair or light.

She put her camera on the seat beside her, wondering why anyone would choose to rent that place. It was at the very end of Water Street, only a few hundred yards from where the cliff met the sea. No beach access. Not that Rocky Point had a lot of beaches. The reason for its name had come from the cliffs meeting the Atlantic. Carlisle Beach was the closest one of any size and it was down the coast by a couple of miles.

She'd ask around. Maybe someone knew who he was.

Allie was tired by the time she reached home, the small converted garage behind a large house that stood vacant more months than it was occupied. The Saverinson family had owned the dwelling for generations. The current family lived in Boston and only came up for the summer months. Since Labor Day had passed a few weeks ago, it would remain empty until next May.

In exchange for living in the converted garage, Allie kept an eye on the house, and made sure the place was cleaned once a month during the winter months. The arrangement suited her to a tee. Her family had hesitated when she'd insisted on moving out eight years ago. They'd wanted to cosset her and keep her safe.

She'd insisted. Life was an adventure and she wanted to enjoy every moment. She wasn't on the path she once thought she'd take, but she was more than satisfied with the life she now had. Much as she loved her mom and dad, they would have stifled her beyond belief if she lived with them. They still saw her as their precious little girl. Emphasis on *little*.

After the car crash that had so drastically changed everything, they were loath to let her out of their sight. She had not died as the others had. Granted, the long months of recuperation and physical therapy had taken their toll, but she had wanted freedom and independence as she'd grown into her twenties.

She'd made the concession of calling almost every day. In the end, her parents had eased up on some of their obsessive need to watch over her all the time.

She didn't believe they blamed themselves for the church van's being hit by that drunk driver. But they did rehash if they should have let her go on the outing. But who would have suspected a tragedy when the youth leader was taking the church group on a field trip to Portland?

Taking the stairs was never easy, but she wouldn't change a thing about her home. At least she could get up and down without too much discomfort. Ten years was plenty long enough to get used to the limitations the accident had imposed. And find ways around them. Entering her home, she shed her camera and jacket, flexing her fingers to loosen them up. It would be pleasantly warm later in the day, but at dawn the fall air was decidedly cool. She grabbed a quick cup of coffee warming in the kitchen, then, grabbing the camera case, she headed for the room where she did most of her work. She couldn't wait to see the pictures she'd taken. She hoped at least one shot came out just as she wanted it.

Without hesitation, she plunged into the day's work.

* * *

Jack Donner watched as Allie Turner's car headed toward town. What in the world had she been doing on the cliffs at dawn? Or at all? She had a bit of a lopsided gait, using her cane to steady herself as she walked. He'd seen her the last three mornings and still didn't know what compelled her to venture over the edge. Maybe one day, he'd ask.

He leaned against the post and turned his gaze to the sea. He should have done more than acknowledge her presence. He could have called hello. Asked what she was doing this morning. Offered her a cup of hot coffee.

He frowned. Small talk was a skill he'd never mastered.

And hadn't needed during the tours of duty in far off Iraq and Afghanistan. It came easy to some. For a moment he tried to imagine himself chatting with other people. He shook his head. It was beyond him.

He was a dedicated soldier, not one for sitting around shooting the breeze. Unless it was with other soldiers. Men he could relate to, learn from.

Scratch that.

He *had been* a dedicated soldier.

Until the unexpected IED.

Until irreversible injuries had rendered him unfit for duty.

Now he had another day to get through. Another fifty years or so to wonder what to do with the rest of his life.

He hadn't ever talked directly with Allie Turner. But he'd seen her every week when she'd arrived at the VA hospital, bringing sunshine and light into the routine that threatened to drive everyone crazy. She had several favorite soldiers she always visited. After she'd left, the men would talk about her visit and the latest stories from the town of Rocky Point, Maine.

While feigning indifference, he'd listened as attentively as the next guy. She'd spoken of a world as foreign to him as Iraq had been. Small town America. Of families who had lived and worked in the area for generations. People who knew their neighbors, banded together in tough times. Celebrated the holidays with traditions that had been handed down for decades.

He shook his head slowly.

Yet here he was, lured to Rocky Point from the stories she'd told. What would she think if she ever found out he'd come here because of her? He'd wanted to see the town that sounded like it should be in a movie. He wanted to find out if there was a place for him in the too-good-to-be-true town of Rocky Point, Maine.

So far it wasn't looking good. He'd been here a week and, except for one venture to the grocery store and a visit to the local clinic to hand over his records, he hadn't left the place. He knew he should make an effort to meet someone beside the doctor and nurse, but the solitude suited him. And small talk was never his thing.

Maybe tomorrow, he'd ask her what she was doing going down the cliff each morning. Acknowledge her with more than a casual nod. Start with Allie Turner. She was the reason he was here.

* * *

Allie was delighted with the pictures when the last one came from her printer. She chose the third in the series to complete the annual report. It was just as she envisioned before she'd begun her morning trek. She'd finalize the camera-ready art today and send the complete packet to the company for approval, and then it'd be put on hold until the year end numbers were ready to slot into spaces left for them, then it'd be off to the printer. One more job crossed off until next year.

She stretched and shrugged her shoulders. Time for a

break. She was surprised to find it was after one o'clock. She knew she lost track of time when working, but having had breakfast so early, she'd expected to be hungry before now.

She wandered into the kitchen and opened the refrigerator door. Nothing looked appealing. Actually, there wasn't much there at all. She wrinkled her nose.

"Forgot I was supposed to go shopping today," she murmured aloud as she slowly closed the refrigerator door. "It's a bad thing to shop on an empty stomach. The perfect excuse to eat at Marcie's." She loved eating at the family coffee shop on Main Street. Since most of the summer visitors had gone home, she knew anyone there today was likely to be someone she knew. She'd catch up on news and enjoy a good meal at the same time.

And maybe find someone who knew who had rented the Stafford place.

Thirty minutes later Allie sat in a booth, awaiting the shrimp po'boy sandwich she'd ordered. The hum of conversation swirled around. Several people had greeted her when she'd arrived, and she'd stopped for a minute or two at their tables before taking the booth the waitress had shown her to. She enjoyed the comfortable air of the café. Even though the summer tourists had left, the waitresses at Marcie's place continued to wear the period dresses from Revolutionary War days. The entire atmosphere of the café mimicked that period and was a great favorite with visitors.

"Hi, Allie, how're you doing?" Marcie stopped by the table. She had run the café for several years and knew everyone in town.

"Couldn't be better. How are things going with you? Getting ready for your big day?"

Marcie nodded, her smile dreamy. "It's a lot of work. I'm glad I helped with Gillian's wedding so I know the ins and outs. I thought hers went perfectly. I want mine to be the same. A winter wedding's chancier, I know, because of the weather. But still—if it's to be, it will be perfect."

"I've always thought a wedding's a wonderful thing, but it's the marriage that needs to be perfect," Allie teased.

Marcie laughed and slipped onto the bench opposite Allie. The owner of the family-style café had recently become engaged to her high school sweetheart. They'd both been part of the wedding party at her fiance's brother's wedding a week after Labor Day. Now the next town wedding would be Marcie's.

"When will Gillian's wedding album be ready?" Marcie asked.

"Shouldn't Gillian be asking that?" Allie teased. She'd been hired as the wedding photographer and had some stunning photos of the bride, the newly-wed couple, and the entire wedding party. It had been a lovely event on a lovely day.

"She'll be asking as soon as she sees you."

"I told her I'd have all the proofs for her when she got back from their honeymoon. They're all finished. I'm ready when she is. Once she settles on which ones she wants, it'll just take a couple of days to complete the album."

"I'd want to see mine as soon as I got back," Marcie said with a grin.

"I'll remember that," Allie said with a smile. She loved

photographing weddings the best of all her various projects.

Marcie would make as pretty a bride as Gillian had. A glow of love radiated from her. Allie shared in the happiness of her friend with just the slightest pang.

She wished she'd fall in love again someday. She tried not to be envious when her friends found the loves of their lives but couldn't help thinking she'd missed out. It seemed unlikely after all these years that she'd find someone in Rocky Point. She'd never met a man she felt that way about since Jason. She had dated from time to time—but rarely more than two or three times with anyone. Her friend Rachel was always urging her to find a guy—even setting her up with a blind date once. There had been no spark and she declined further offers from her friend.

No one caught her fancy. And she didn't want to be a burden to some man who might like to hike or do other physical activities. The accident had killed Jason, permanently handicapped her, and devastated the entire community. Maybe the Lord had her on this path to show others they could be happy and fulfilled without being married.

When the waitress served lunch, she also brought a cup of coffee for Marcie. After Allie had taken several bites of the sandwich, she remembered to ask Marcie if she knew who'd rented the Staffords' home.

"That old place at the end of Water Street?"

Allie nodded. "I've seen lights on the last couple of days really early when I was out on a shoot. Today I saw a man standing on the porch when I went by. I was surprised as it's long past the season. You haven't seen any strangers in town?"

"What were you photographing from the end of that street?" Marcie asked, intrigued.

"I wanted the green flash."

"And that is?" Marcie asked.

"The burst of green along the horizon when the sun is coming up out of the sea."

Marcie laughed. "Yeah, like the sun comes out of the sea. Didn't you learn more about astronomy when you were in school?"

"You know what I mean. I wanted it for an annual report I'm working on. I've been going there several mornings to try for the perfect shot. I got it today," she said with satisfaction.

Marcie shook her head. "I haven't a clue who rented the old house. Summer visitors are gone for the most part. We can expect a few coming in for the fall colors, but I can't say I've seen any strangers in the last few days. That house isn't exactly a highly sought after property, even in the high season. It needs a lot of work, plus who needs five bedrooms these days? Ask Tate, if you see him. He keeps abreast of who's new in town."

Tate Johnson was the Sheriff of the town and county and made sure he knew what was going on. He'd been born and raised in Rocky Point and knew everyone.

"It's not that important, I just wondered," Allie said. She wanted to be neighborly, but not pester the Sheriff with something like that. Anyway, did it really matter? Mostly it had her curiosity up a notch.

"I'll ask, then. I'm curious myself," Marcie said, nodding toward the door as Tate Johnson entered.

She beckoned him over and Tate made his way around the tables to Marcie and Allie, stopping to say hi when someone called to him.

"Come for some pie?" Marcie asked, slipping out of the booth.

"Just some coffee. Allie." He greeted her.

"Have a seat and I'll get you a cup. We have a question for you," Marcie said, heading over to where the coffee was kept.

"Problem?" Tate asked Allie, as he slid into the space Marcie had been.

"No, just curiosity. I'll wait for Marcie so you can tell us both if you know."

"Intriguing," he said, resting his hat on the bench beside him.

When Marcie settled in beside Allie after giving Tate a steaming cup of coffee, she looked at Allie. "Did you ask?

"I waited for you." She turned to Tate. "I was out at the end of Water Street this morning and saw the Stafford house is occupied. Know who's renting it?"

He took a sip of coffee and looked at them. "Sure. Jack Donner. I'm surprised you don't know him, Allie. He was most recently in the VA hospital in Portland. Just released a week ago. Checked in with doc when he got to town. Strong enough to leave the hospital, but still needs watching is my guess."

"Which explains how you know about him," Marcie said, referring to Tate's contact at the clinic. His fiancee was the clinic's nurse.

He shrugged. "I'm not telling you anything confidential. Faith told me he'd checked in there, brought medical records. Plans to stay in town for a while anyway. You ever see him at the hospital?"

Allie slowly shook her head. "I don't place the name. I usually visit with the same guys each time and he's not one of them."

Allie had started visiting the veteran's hospital when one of the local boys had been sent there after receiving injuries in Iraq. She'd continued after Connor was released, since there were so many men there who didn't have family who could visit. Her once a week visits were special and she liked knowing she brought a change to the routine for those men who had put their lives on the line.

"Maybe I'll take him some cookies," she murmured, wondering if she'd recognize him when she saw him up close. There were always men in the community room that didn't join her group.

"Take chocolate chip cookies, they're my favorite," Tate murmured. "I love the ones Faith makes."

"You love anything Faith makes," Marcie said. "How's her dog doing?"

"Really well. She's picked up obedience training as if she was made for it. She can go for her walks without being on a leash, and I don't worry about her dragging Faith along."

The three of them chatted, until Marcie had to go answer a question another diner had and Tate finished his coffee and said he had to be going.

Once she was finished eating, Allie headed for the grocery store. Mid-afternoon was usually a quiet time to shop. She had an arrangement with the local store to have her groceries delivered once she purchased them. Young Josh Diggs was the kid who usually brought them. He was always careful with eggs and other fragile items, which she appreciated.

She hung her cane on the cart and used the handle to help her balance. Slowly she walked up one aisle and down the other putting items in the cart, trying to plan a few meals in her mind so she could get what she needed ahead of time.

Rounding the corner, she almost bumped into another cart.

"Oh, sorry." She looked up and into the deepest blue eyes she'd ever seen. She blinked. That wasn't quite right. She'd seen these eyes before–at the VA hospital.

"Oh, it's you. You're out," she said in surprise.

The man nodded, turning his head slightly. "You make it sound as if I escaped from prison."

Allie laughed. "Hardly. It's wonderful they released you. What are you doing here in Rocky Point?"

He hesitated a moment, then said, "I've rented a place. I'll finish recuperating here. It's close enough I can get to the hospital if I need to, yet away from Portland. Quiet. Peaceful."

"You're not from around here are you? I thought I knew of all the men from town who were in the military."

"No. I'm not from around here."

Allie waited a moment, but he wasn't more forthcoming. "I'm Allie Turner," she said offering her hand.

Again he hesitated, then took hers in his left hand. "Jack Donner."

She couldn't help looking at his right hand, resting on the handle of the cart. Racking her brain to remember what she knew about this man, she came up with virtually nothing. She'd seen him in the large community television room at the hospital when she'd visited the men she considered her regulars. Actually, she'd first noticed Jack several months ago. At that time he'd been in a wheelchair, sitting at a table of four, playing cards, a scowl on his face. She also remembered seeing him at a table a month ago—no wheelchair, same scowl. She hadn't realized how tall he was. There were scars showing along his right cheek and neck. Had his arm been injured so badly he couldn't shake hands?

"Welcome to Rocky Point."

"Thanks."

She waited a moment but he didn't say another word.

"Well, I'm in the phone book, so give me a call if you need anything," she said brightly. He probably had a whole slew of relatives and friends to look out for him. Still, she didn't see anyone with him today. Maybe he cherished his independence as much as she did.

She knew better than most how cloying and smothering concern could be while struggling to regain as much of a normal life as possible.

Jack nodded.

Allie pushed her cart around his, searching for the next item on her mental list, resisting the temptation to turn around to see him again.

She was almost at the end of the aisle when she gave in and looked over her shoulder. He was reading the label of a box. She should have done more. Said something more. Maybe invited him to coffee or something. Maybe she would take him those cookies she talked about as a welcome to Rocky Point. Watching for him as she completed her shopping she was disappointed she didn't see him again. He must have been going through the store in the opposite direction from her.

She arranged for Josh to deliver her groceries and started for home. She included a bag of chocolate chips. Then she debated. It was only being neighborly. Was it too pushy? He hadn't seemed happy to see her. Yet he was a stranger in town. It would be friendly. Rocky Point was a friendly town. She'd do it.

Maybe.

He probably had tons of friends and relatives around.

It wouldn't hurt to show some hospitality.

If he wasn't from around here, why had he come to Rocky Point to recuperate? He could have found a place closer to the hospital if he needed continued care from the VA.

She wasn't home ten minutes before Josh knocked on the door.

"Afternoon, Allie," he said, entering her house with a bag in each arm.

"Hi, Josh. Thanks for bringing my stuff," she said, opening the door wide and letting him go right to the kitchen and put the bags on one of the counters.

"Be right back with the rest," he said. When he deposited the last of the bags of groceries, he turned to her.

"Remember me telling you about getting on Zack Kincaid's driving program?"

"I do. How's that going?" Josh had shared his excitement at taking driving lessons from a noted Grand Prix driver like Zack Kincaid, when Zack had decided to open a course for teens in a nearby town.

"Really good! The fact is on Saturday, we're having like an open house. To show off what's been done for the track, and to show off some of what we're learning. Zack won't let us race around the track, but he'll be talking to everyone about what we plan. Anyway, I wondered if you wanted to come to see it. My mom said she could give you a ride."

"I'd love to. I'll bring my camera and try to get some good pictures."

Josh nodded. "My mom said she could come by around nine."

"I'll be ready."

Allie put away her groceries, thinking about Josh and the excitement the boys in town evidenced at the new driving track. Zack Kincaid was a world-renowned race car winner and was settling in Rocky Point. He and Marcie would be married later in the year. In the meantime, he'd arranged for an old factory's parking lot to be leased to him and he was setting up a driving school. Allie knew the Sheriff had been part of the group making recommendations in favor of the project. Good school work was required of all who wanted to be part of the new start up. Josh updated her each time he delivered her groceries. To the teens in town, this was an amazing opportunity.

She'd take her camera and see if she could capture some action shots. Maybe do a short article for the local paper to let others in town know how the endeavor was going. Planning for Saturday, she put away the groceries and then took out the ingredients for cookies.

* * *

Jack picked up the thin phone book. There couldn't be more than seventy pages in the entire thing. He shook his head. He didn't know towns like this really existed. At least not before he'd started listening to Allie when she'd visited the VA hospital.

He found Allie's number in the directory as she'd said. He started to dial, then replaced the receiver. What was he going to say? She was probably being polite in the store—telling him her name was in the book and call if he needed anything.

He didn't need anything.

Well, he'd like his life back as it had been. But that was never going to happen.

So why was he thinking of calling her? He didn't go out if he could help it. Grocery shopping had been the limit of his excursions since he'd arrived in Rocky Point last week. That and the clinic.

He hated the way people stared at the scars. And the shock if he didn't shake hands like normal men. Hated not being able to hear clearly like before. Or have the stamina or energy to not need a nap every day. Sometimes he felt like a little kid–it was not a feeling he relished.

Too bad Rocky Point was too small for a Starbucks. That would be easier. Grab a cup, find a table–his mind went blank. Even if she joined him for a cup of joe, what would they talk about?

Maybe he wouldn't have to say much. When he'd seen her at the VA hospital, he'd watch her tell the men stories about Rocky Point. Allie's love for her town and neighbors always sounded like a dream. One he secretly yearned for. Only soldiers didn't yearn for things–except keep their men safe and defeat the enemy.

Now that he was here, he was as isolated as he had been in the hospital. If he ever wanted part of the dream life she spoke about, he had to move forward. Think of it as a military campaign, he tried to tell himself. Study, plan, infiltrate.

For a moment he closed his eyes, seeing himself back at camp with his men. Complaining about the heat and the sand and the bugs. Counting the days until the deployment was over and they'd head back to the States. He knew where he stood with soldiers. Not so much with civilians. He'd gone into the Army after high school graduation. For twelve years it had been his life. One he'd liked.

What could he say to Allie if he called her? What would she say if he asked her out for coffee? One reason he wanted to be in Rocky Point was to find the life she talked about, if it was even there. Hiding in the house wouldn't get him far. Soldiers did things whether they were scared or not–always moving forward. Holding that thought, he lifted the receiver and dialed before he could change his mind.

The phone rang. And rang. He was about to hang up when she answered, breathlessly.

"Hi, it's Jack Donner."

"Oh, hi. I had to run for the phone. I was in the back working. I really should get a phone back there, or remember to take this one with me."

Great, he was interrupting her. "I can call back," he offered.

"It's okay. Nothing critical. I'm working on some copies of photos I took this morning. Trying different crops to see which is the most dramatic."

"You're a photographer?" Funny, he'd pictured her as a writer. She had a way with words when talking about her neighbors and friends that painted a picture in his mind that wouldn't let go. Now he remembered he'd seen some sort of case slung over her shoulder that morning. Had she been taking pictures at the crack of dawn?

"I am. A photographer of everything from weddings, to school events, to annual reports," she replied.

"Was that why you were on the cliffs this morning?" he asked.

"That was me. I went down the rocks a short distance to be closer to the horizon for the shot—I was looking for the green flash for a back cover of an annual report for SeaRovers Inc."

"Green flash?" He frowned. What was a green flash?

Allie explained and while he listened, Jack could picture her animation. She moved her hands when she talked, did she know that? Her face lit up and seemed to sparkle. Even through the phone he could hear her enthusiasm. She seemed to face life like that all the time.

"Isn't it early for an annual report?" he asked when she ran down. He didn't know much about business, but wasn't December the end of the year and time for the annual report after that?

"That's the cool thing about this company; they get all their ducks in a row early. They don't have the year-end financial reports, of course. That's months away. But when they do, they'll be ready to go. I wish some of my other clients would do things before the last minute."

"Maybe you should tell them."

She laughed. "Yeah. They're the clients, they're always right. How long are you going to be in Rocky Point? How did you even hear about the Stafford place? It's a bit off the beaten path, you know. What brought you here?"

He had no plans. But he wouldn't tell her that.

"I asked for a quiet place. The realtor showed me this one. It's not expensive."

"I should hope not the condition it's in."

"What's wrong with it? I was assured the roof doesn't leak. It's got a great view and no noisy neighbors."

"So what are you doing here in town?"

Nothing. He gazed out the window at the sea. "Recuperating, I said that."

Someone like Allie wouldn't want to know the doctors thought he was about as right as he was going to get. They had a few follow up visits scheduled, but for the most part, he was done. The only recuperating he'd be doing was trying to get some more muscle strength in his right hand and arm. He hadn't a single plan for finding some kind of work. Who wanted a half deaf, half incapacitated man to do anything? All he knew was the military. He wasn't sure he could make the transition to civilian life.

"I'm on disability," he said at last. He hated the fact, and hated having to say it. But there was nothing more to be done until he'd had time for the muscles to heal and strengthen. Then the doctors would be able to assess if he was fit for some kind of work, or destined to be a semi invalid the rest of his life.

Sometimes he wondered why the IED hadn't finished the job.

"Injured in Iraq?" The soft sympathy in her voice touched him. He frowned. He'd survived. Others hadn't. She should save her sympathy for them and their families.

"Afghanistan."

"Well, you must be on the road to recovery for the hospital to discharge you," she said brightly.

Did she always have such a rosy view of things? He hesitated. It was one of the things that appealed to him. Allie saw life as a delight. He saw it as something to slog through.

"They can't do any more for me, so they kicked me out," he said, summing up what he felt.

She laughed. Jack almost smiled. Her laughter was infectious. He remembered that from when he'd listened to her at the hospital. It had interrupted the card game. The others had looked at her, taking in her pretty curly auburn hair, the green eyes that sparkled clear across the room. One of the men had wondered aloud what she was laughing over. He'd always wondered himself.

"You have someone you visit at the VA?" he asked. Was it a boyfriend? Relative?

"I visit several men—Tom McGurk, Paul Williams and Solly Cameretti."

"They from Rocky Point?" he asked. He knew Solly slightly. And he was from Brooklyn.

"Nope. I met them when I volunteered to visit every week—I asked for men who didn't have relatives nearby."

"Why?"

"Why what?"

"Never mind. It's not my business. Why choose those who don't have relatives nearby?" he contradicted himself in one sentence. He didn't have relatives at all, much less nearby. What if she'd started visiting him? He hadn't asked for anything; didn't want pity or charity. He'd learned to stand on his own years ago. No ties, no baggage.

But he wanted to hear her talk, hear her laugh. He liked the fact someone in the world was so optimistic and happy.

"We had a young boy from town die in Iraq. We all took it hard. Then another—Conner--was wounded and sent to the VA hospital for recovery. He goes to my church, so I went up to visit. I began to wonder about those who are there when family and friends are too far away to visit. When I talked to the pastor at my church, he suggested asking at the hospital if there was any need. So I found out they liked visitors. It's boring to be stuck in hospital for weeks and months on end. So I started about three years ago."

He remembered her awkward gait as she walked along the road. She'd had something cause that limp. Had she been months in hospital? Days when she thought she might not walk again? Nights to get through when the pain kept her awake?

"Mmm." Calling had been a mistake. He had nothing left to say. How could he get out of this without seeming like an idiot?

"I saw you there," she said easily.

He knew that from her comment at the store. But it still surprised him that she'd noticed him. He'd never spoken to her before today.

"I was there five months."

"And now you're out. And here in town." She was silent a moment and he was about to say goodbye when she said,

"How about some chocolate chip cookies. I made some. The last batch is still warm."

"What?"

"I know where you live. I could zip over there with a plate. You can tell me about why you chose to move here, and I'll tell you all I know about Rocky Point. You have chairs on the porch, right? It's still warm enough to sit outside. I love Indian summer. Cold at night, warm in the day."

Two things registered simultaneously—he didn't have to go out in public and she wanted to see him.

"I like chocolate chip cookies," Jack said. He remembered when men in his platoon received care packages from home. Sometimes cookies were included and they shared.

He'd wanted to come to Rocky Point because of her.

Now he wondered if that had been a smart move. He wasn't ready to interact with others. He might never be ready. One reason this house had suited him was its isolation. He didn't have any near neighbors. Yet here she was, inviting herself over.

"Me, too. So you're there alone? Or should I bring more than a couple of dozen?"

Who else would be here with him? He had no family. All his friends were in the military. Yes, he was here in Rocky Point on his own. And likely to remain that way if he didn't make an effort to start getting to know people.

Study, plan, infiltrate. "There's no one else here."

When he hung up, Jack leaned back on the sofa. He massaged the constant ache in his right arm absently with his left hand as he considered how easily he could make a complete fool of himself. He should have left well enough alone. Now Allie would come over, find he couldn't talk intelligently about much besides different ordnance or strategic planning. She'd leave and he'd probably never see her again unless he ran into her at the store.

He knew Solly looked forward to her visits. He'd often repeated the stories Allie had told them. Jack admitted to being a touch envious. No one had visited him the entire time he'd been at the hospital. Not that he expected anyone to. What friends he still had were still at war. When they returned to the States, they'd be heading to military bases throughout the country. None would be coming to Portland.

Resting his head back on the cushions, he gazed at the ceiling. Solly was most likely going to stay there for another six months or longer. Or be transferred to a long-term care facility closer to Brooklyn. He wasn't going to walk out one day.

In that respect, Jack guessed he was luckier than others. But he missed the men in his unit. He missed the camaraderie they shared. They'd been close—as close as brothers—until the IED had killed Ham and Rosco and injured him so badly. Now the survivors had a new platoon leader, still on deployment to Afghanistan. While he was in some small Maine town, where he had a nodding acquaintance with one person.

And a bleak limited future stretching out ahead of him. After today.

Today he was going to see Allie Turner again, and for a few moments, the world would be a brighter place.

Chapter Two

Allie drove slowly, wanting to arrive without dumping the cookies on the floor. When she reached the Stafford place, she saw Jack sitting on the porch.

"Hi," she called when she opened the door. With one hand holding her cane, it was hard to reach back in and pick up and balance the plate of cookies. She hadn't made it all the way here to spill them before they were enjoyed.

He came to the car and reached out with his left hand to take the plate

Transitioning from sitting to standing was always hard. Once on her feet, she shut the door with her hip.

"Chairs are on the porch, aimed toward the sea," he said walking along beside her.

"You have a great view," she said as she climbed the two wooden steps to the porch. She hesitated when she saw the Adirondacks chairs. Not the easiest things to get out of. Seeing a beat-up stool near the corner, she pulled it over and perched on it.

"Easier for me to get up from," she said in explanation when he looked puzzled.

"I can bring a chair from inside."

"No, this is fine. It's a gorgeous day, isn't it?" The sun was already behind the house, but the ambient temperature remained balmy. The day remained cloudless and had warmed up considerably from the early morning.

"It feels good to me," Jack said, sitting in a chair next to her and offering the plate of cookies.

They each took a cookie and gazed out to the blue sea as they munched in silence. "These are good." They were still warm, the chocolate chips melting on his tongue as he ate.

"Thanks."

"Do you often risk your life for a photograph?" he asked when he'd finished his cookie. "I walked over to the cliff earlier; it's a long way down."

She looked at him and grinned. "Hardly risking my life. I didn't go too far over the top, and I was very careful."

"Looked dangerous from here."

"Mostly I take pictures of people, but sometimes I want to be creative and try something different. I want to keep my customers happy. So, tell me how you like Rocky Point so far?"

He shrugged, then winced. Allie could tell the gesture hurt. She remembered doing the most mundane things when she'd got out of the hospital and the months it had taken her to retrain herself on what she could and couldn't do. She had constantly prayed for patience. She knew the pain from pushing to retrain muscles, the depression she constantly fought over all she'd lost. Had Jack experienced the same feelings?

"I haven't seen much of it yet, mostly the grocery store,

the clinic and the view from this porch," he said.

"Well, you came at a good time. There's a lot to do in the fall, even though most of the tourists have left. We all support the high school football team–going out to watch the games when they're played in town. Some of us go to the away games as well. I usually do, since I'm helping the seniors take pictures for the yearbook. Then in winter we have basketball. The church has some activities: Harvest Festival and Christmas, of course. There are Bible study classes, and choir and socials throughout the winter months."

She tried to gauge Jack's reaction. He watched her as she spoke, but she couldn't tell if any of the activities interested him or not.

"And--Zack Kincaid's started a driving school. A bunch of us are going over there on Saturday to see it. It's open house day. One of his kids invited me. Want to go?"

"To a driving school?"

Allie smiled again, reaching for another cookie. She was gratified when he did as well.

"I don't know anything about it, that's why I'm going to see it. Zack's some fancy Grand Prix race driver, so my guess is this isn't going to be boring. Come with me; you can meet some more people. If you're planning to stay a while. Are you?"

Jack shrugged. "I have no idea."

"Oh. Well." She began nibbling around the edge of the cookie. "When will you know?"

"Know what?"

"If you're going to stay. Is this just temporary until you

get back into active duty?"

He shook his head. "I'm never going back to active duty."

She heard the bitterness in his tone and her heart went out to him. She'd heard that tone with other soldiers in the VA hospital, angry at the way things had turned out, bitter they wouldn't be returning to the career they'd loved. She could relate a little: hadn't her own life been forever changed? But through God's grace, she'd been able to find work she loved, a place of her own and friends who accepted her--limitations and all.

"So what are you going to do next?" she asked gently.

He stared out across the ocean, the only sound the muffled waves of the sea beating on the cliff.

"Grow old and die, I guess," he said after a long moment.

Allie looked at him in startled surprise. "There's too much to enjoy in life to feel that way. You have years of life ahead of you."

He looked at her, glancing at her cane. "You must have thought that way once or twice. What happened to you? You weren't born needing a cane."

"I was in a bad car crash; the church minivan was T-boned by a drunk driver. It changed everything," she replied quietly. Everyone in town had been impacted by the horrible accident when she'd been a teenager. Her family, friends and neighbors had been so solicitous and supportive. Too much so, sometimes. It was feeling smothered with love that had had her insisting she needed her own place, her own career.

"Sorry," he mumbled.

"Way in the past. And I was lucky, the only survivor." Though so often in those early days she hadn't felt lucky. She'd never understood why she'd been spared and the other teens from her youth group had been killed. Especially Jason.

She could still see his grin, hear the echo of his voice when she thought about him in the night. They'd been so in love, so sure they had a bright future together.

He nodded. "The IED that ended my career took out two of the men in the vehicle with me. Sometimes I wonder why I wasn't killed instead. I have no family, no kids. They were both married and had children. Yet here I am, and they're dead."

"No one knows the ways of God, only He does. But I think He has a plan for each of us. One that we can't see at the time. I'm hoping when I get old, I can look back and see why things happened and what I did that made a difference."

Jack finished his cookie and leaned his head against the high back of the Adirondack chair. "Can't see any great plan in getting fathers killed. I grew up without one; it sucks."

Allie couldn't respond. She knew life wasn't always easy or fair. Jason wouldn't have died if life was fair. Her boyfriend had been accepted to Harvard, was planning to become a doctor. She had planned on a nursing career. Their dream had been to join Doctors Without Borders and serve in places that normally didn't have quality medical care.

That dream had ended when Jason was killed and she was crippled.

Jack looked at Allie as she perched on the stool, her cane

leaning against the wall of the house. The chaplain at the VA hospital had talked to him more than once about God being in charge, and that His ways weren't the ways of men. Jack still didn't see the reason why good men were killed and bad ones roamed the earth.

Had it been a plan of God's for him to come to Rocky Point? He'd thought it was for Allie. He liked looking at her. She was like springtime: fresh and optimistic and full of joy. He didn't know her background, but could imagine how horrendous the crash must have been that she was the only survivor–and wound up using a cane. The surprise was, it hadn't made her bitter.

He was trying not to let what happened to him make him bitter, but that was hard to do. He didn't want to be handicapped for the rest of his life. He was a soldier. It was all he knew.

"So want to go to see Zack's driving set up on Saturday?" she asked again.

He didn't want to do anything. He wanted to get back to the way he'd been. Had coming here been a mistake?

"Come on, you'll be able to meet some more people, get into the swing of things in Rocky Point," she urged. "And maybe you'd like to come to Trinity Church on Sunday. There's a young adult group that's a lot of fun."

"I'll think about it." And come up with a no if she asked again. The thought of mingling with strangers, having to explain over and over what had happened, trying to hear what was going on with his hearing loss almost paralyzed him.

"Let me know before Saturday. I've been offered a ride,

but if you go, I'll drive."

"Go with your friend." He wondered who had invited her. Some guy, probably. He looked out toward the sea.

"Nope, I think it'll do you a world of good. Let's plan to leave before nine. I want the full day at the track."

She hesitated a moment, and Jack looked back to see why.

"Unless a full day would be too much. You aren't long out of the hospital." Her expression was of concern, not pity.

"I don't have full use of my right arm. Can't hear out of the right ear and have hearing loss in the left one. And I won't ever walk like I did, though I'm as well as I'm going to get, the doctors said. I could do a whole day." Bravado talking. He hadn't made it an entire day in the solitude of the house without needing to lie down before he fell down. Who did he think he was, committing to a full day of the stress of meeting people, trying to be as normal as they were when he knew he never again would be? Trying to hear, trying to fit in conversations where he heard only one word in three.

Her smile dazzled him. "Great, I'll pick you up at eight-thirty. Unless you want an earlier start—we could have breakfast at the café. Marcie's a friend of mine, and I often splurge on the weekend and have a meal there. Actually, I splurge a lot and eat there often. The food's good and it's not so much fun cooking for one."

"Seeing the race car driver and his set up will be enough." So much for refusing.

"Marcie'll be there, too, I expect. She's engaged to Zack.

They're having a Christmas wedding and I'm taking the pictures." She smiled and reached for her cane. "I need to take off. I have more stuff to do so I can goof off tomorrow."

He rose when she did. He'd committed to going, though he'd thought he'd have found a way out of it by now. Yet he couldn't say anything that would dampen the bright smile of expectation she wore.

"Thanks for the cookies."

"Glad you enjoyed them." She used her cane to get down the shallow wooden steps to the walkway.

He followed, conscious of the limitations that would be forever with him. He wanted to say something. To keep her talking a little longer. But he wasn't up on small talk, and couldn't think of a reason that didn't sound totally stupid to keep her here.

"See you Saturday," she said with a wave and smile.

In only minutes, Jack stood alone on his weathered porch, feeling the breeze from the sea with the salt tang. Saturday. It was two days away. He stared out over the blue waters and wondered what he'd do to kill time for two days.

* * *

Jack rose early on Saturday, anticipation building despite his attempts to keep any feelings at bay. At least his routine would change today. He'd see Allie again.

And have to face who knew how many strangers, endure their stares, the curiosity that had been so rampant when he'd made forays into Portland. At least at the hospital, everyone had known why they were there. Some weren't ever leaving the care facilities. He should be glad he was capable of living on his own.

Except he still didn't know what to do with the rest of his life.

Take one day at a time, his buddies had said. That's all any of them could do.

He was ready to go long before eight thirty. He felt as nervous as a teenager taking out a girl he had a crush on. He thought back to those days. His teen years had been especially hard. He'd been in three different foster homes for his four years of high school. The uncertainty of never knowing from one week to the next if he'd be changing schools had had him keeping more to himself. It had been better not to form attachments than to have to say goodbye with hardly any notice. He'd always been conscious that other teens had stable families, longtime friends. Even long term girl and boyfriends. He'd felt as if he'd been on the outside looking in at something he could never attain.

He had fared better once he'd joined the military. Then he'd known how long the duty assignment was, could make friends, date. Establish some long term career goals. Focus on his duty and responsibilities. He had a future he liked and could deal with.

All that was changed now.

He could still call her and refuse to go. He'd debated doing that a dozen times since she'd left. But unless he wanted to become a hermit, he had to make a foray into the real world some time. And who better to be introduced around by than someone like Allie.

She'd changed her plans to take him. He couldn't back out at this late a date. Sighing for the day ahead, he went to stand on the porch, a cup of coffee in hand. He liked the serenity of the house. He couldn't see another dwelling from the porch. The isolation suited him. No need to worry about noisy neighbors or worse, curious ones.

The house needed a lot of work, but the owners didn't seem to care. It was well lived in, the furniture past its prime. Still, it was comfortable and clean. He'd seen the upstairs bedrooms, but chosen the only one on the ground floor–it had a great view of the sea and was the largest one in the house. There was one bath down and one up. An old worn kitchen. But the view couldn't be beat. And for all the cooking he did, the kitchen suited. It was mostly heating things up, or plain and simple meals.

It was cool in the early morning, but the light jacket he wore was enough. He'd probably shed it by midday. Indian summer lingered and it felt good. Being outside felt good after months in the hospital. He didn't believe he'd ever take another day for granted.

When he saw Allie's SUV, he put the cup on the railing and headed down the stairs. No sense having her get out of the car. He wasn't looking forward to getting in or out himself. Yet the large, sturdy vehicle would be easier to manoeuver in than some small compact. And he knew the four wheel drive had to be handy in the winter with the snow that accumulated.

"Good morning," she greeted him, smiling broadly when

he opened the passenger side door. At least she'd be on his hearing side during the drive.

"Good morning," he replied formally.

"I saw your friend Solly at the VA yesterday," she said, as she backed out of the drive and headed back toward town. "He said you're a lucky son of a gun, and don't forget your friends there now that you're out. If you'd like to go up with me sometime, I'd be glad for the company."

"Umm." He stared out the window. The last thing he wanted was to go back if he didn't need to. Yet the thought of the men whom he'd passed the time with for months made him reconsider. He knew how the routine dragged. How staring endlessly at the pale walls could almost drive a man crazy.

"Yeah, sure, let me know."

"I visit almost every Friday. How about next week?" she asked.

"I'll see." Like he needed to check a calendar or something. He had nothing to do, he knew that already.

He watched as she bypassed the town and took a highway inland. Glancing at Allie, he wondered if he should say something, or if it was normal for her to have periods of silence. He had nothing to say, so gazed at the scenery.

"The car course is on a huge parking lot of a manufacturing plant that went bankrupt years ago. It was just sitting there when Zack came up with his idea for a driving school. The high school kids are wild about it. And he doesn't limit participation to only Rocky Point kids, but has them enrolled from all around the area. This is their first open house. The place is just starting. I'm excited to see it. They even rented portable bleachers so we can have good seats when they demo their driving exercises."

"That's enough for him? A race car driver teaching high school kids?" Had something happened to him to knock him off track? Jack couldn't imagine teaching army exercises to kids being satisfying after being in the front lines.

"Well, he also helps his brother in vintage car repairs. And he's getting married. He said settling down with Marcie makes everything worthwhile. I think that's so romantic."

Jack glanced at her. She had that dreamy-eyed expression some women got when they thought about weddings.

"You're not married, I take it," he said. Why had he not thought of that question before?

"No." The dreamy eyed look vanished.

He waited for something more, but she didn't say a word. Was it a touchy subject? If she asked him, he'd say he was single and planning to stay that way. He was sure marriage was not for him. It had not been for his father, who had deserted his mother when Jack was still in diapers. He hadn't stayed the course. Nor returned when his mother had died and he was left to the foster care system. The best way to not worry about repeating history was to stay away from marriage. He'd never been tempted. The military had been his whole life.

That was gone. Still no reason to change his life-long belief that he was destined to remain single. Good thing. He couldn't imagine a wife being happy to have a semi invalid for a husband. It would be like having another kid under foot.

Most women wanted marriage—at least he thought so. And someone as pretty and friendly as Allie: he'd have thought she would have been married for years. What was wrong with the men in Rocky Point?

"We're almost there," she said a short time later. He watched as the traffic increased from virtually no cars to a half dozen. Then he saw the large asphalt parking lot with a high chain-link fence surrounding it. The wide double gates were opened and cars were turning in. There were teenagers everywhere, directing traffic, answering questions when cars stopped beside them. In the distance he saw the portable bleachers she'd mentioned. There were lots more people here than he'd expected—in the hundreds, he'd guess.

Allie stopped near a teen and rolled down her window. "Handicap?" she asked, pointing to the placard on her windshield.

The kid pointed out an area near the bleachers. She thanked him and drove over there. Jack wondered if he'd be gutsy enough to do that, or would pride have him parking like everyone else and then struggling to walk the distance. He said nothing, but was thankful she could park closer.

Theirs was only the second car in the area.

"This is as close as it gets, soldier. We walk from here," she said turning off the engine.

"Not a great distance," he said, studying the area. The bleachers were already half full. With the steady stream of cars turning into the lot, he expected they'd be completely full before the program started.

"Let's hope they have a handicap section so we don't

have to climb a bazillion steps," she said, when he joined her beside the driver's door. Walking so she was on his left side, they headed toward the bleachers.

In less than five minutes they were seated on row two, right in the center. Allie had some pull, he thought, then almost smiled. Charm is what she had. And she shared it with everyone.

They had scarcely sat before people called greetings, some walking over to give her a hug. Jack was amazed at the number of people who knew Allie and stopped to speak to her. She introduced Jack to everyone who stopped. He'd never remember their names, but might recognize faces if he saw them again.

His mind was going numb with all the faces and names. He could tell she was well loved in this community. Again he wondered why she wasn't married. Seemed like she'd make a great mother; she had a hug or kind word to say to all the kids who scrambled over the bleachers to see her. He wasn't sure how old she was, probably a bit younger than he was. Didn't women usually marry earlier?

His thoughts were interrupted when a tall man with dark hair and an easy gait walked out to the microphone set up near the front of the bleachers. Everyone started clapping, whistling and making noise. Obviously the star of the show: Zack Kincaid. Tall with dark hair and eyes, and casual jeans and shirt. He grinned at the applause and waved.

He clicked on the mike.

"Good morning and thanks for coming."

Feet stomped on the bleachers, making a roar that

drowned out his words as everyone continued to clap.

"Thanks for that," he said. At least that's what Jack thought he said. It was hard to hear him. In moments, however, the crowd settled down and grew quiet.

"The kids and I are glad you came for our open house. We have some driving demonstrations to show you, then we invite you to walk the course in groups—the kids have their spiel down pat." Laughter met that statement.

"We've got some cars to sit in and maybe a photo op if you like. But no racing!"

The people laughed again. Allie was beaming as Zack talked. Jack had trouble looking away. She was the prettiest woman he'd ever seen and her enthusiasm for life was contagious. He enjoyed the simple act of watching her. No one here expected anything from him. No one here cared if he could hear well or make small talk. He gradually began to relax and enjoy the activities—as different from his experiences as anything he'd seen.

There was definitely a hierarchy of drivers. Those just learning went first. A course was laid out with bright orange cones. The drivers had to maintain their speed, make the turns and end up parallel parking. Jack winced as kid after kid knocked over a cone here and there, stopped and backed up to try again. Their expressions were so serious. Then the next group came–better, but not perfection yet. The final group aced the course. Then, as a treat for their performance, Zack let them have an impromptu drag race from one area of the lot to the other.

Everyone cheered at each event, and were on their feet

for the drag race.

Allie laughed. "Zack doesn't want it to get around, but he and Tate and Joe were always drag racing out on one of the county back roads. Lucky they didn't kill themselves or anyone else," she said, leaning closer so Jack could hear. "Guess he thought it would be safer to give into their need for speed under supervised control."

He nodded, amazed at what the man had accomplished. He had teenagers following minute directions with no objective but to accomplish the manoeuver. He obviously had the support of families for the supervised activities, and law enforcement if the Sheriff and his deputy, standing to one side clapping as wildly as the rest of the audience, were any indication.

When people began pouring out of the bleacher for the tours, Allie looked at him.

"Tell me true, are you up to a tour?"

"Are you?"

"Always," she said with a wide smile. "I can't wait to see what's going on and how the kids like it."

"I'd think you already have a glimpse of how they like it—they're crazy about it."

"It's good for them, too."

A young man came over. "Hi Allie. I asked to be your tour guide."

"Why, Josh, what a nice thing. Have you met Jack yet?" Her smiled rivaled the sun. Jack knew why the teen wanted to give her the tour. He'd do almost anything to receive a smile like that himself.

Josh held out his hand. For a moment Jack hesitated. This put a damper on things.

He held out his left hand and gripped the kid's for a second.

"Nice to meet you." His foster mom Evelyn would be proud at his manners. She'd tried hard enough to instill them in him.

"Jack just moved here. He was in Afghanistan, injured there and now settling in Rocky Point," Allie said, as she used her cane to help her rise. Jack could see the movement pained her.

"Sorry you got hurt, man. But thanks for your service," Josh said seriously.

Jack was taken aback, touched. No one had ever thanked him for serving. He nodded, suddenly unable to say a word.

"Okay, give us the grand tour. And you'd better believe I want a photo op sitting in that race car of Zack's," Allie said.

Josh had learned the spiel, as Zack had said. He was so enthusiastic Jack envied him. He wished he could find something to make him as enthusiastic about life. They learned about the different driving techniques Zack taught, about the classes he held on safety and accident avoidance.

The best part, according to Allie, was actually sitting in the race car and having her picture taken by one of the teens charged with that duty.

"I'll give you a copy at church tomorrow," the girl said when she'd snapped a couple of photos of Allie. "It's weird taking your picture, Allie."

"You're really getting good in your work, Tricia. I look

forward to seeing the results tomorrow."

"Want to have a shot?" Tricia asked Jack.

"I'll pass this time." He wanted to ask for a copy of the one she'd done of Allie, but didn't know how to without looking like an idiot.

As they started to move on, Tricia touched him lightly on the arm. "Want a copy of Allie's picture, then, as a remembrance of the day?"

He nodded, glancing at the woman walking ahead of him.

"See you in church," the teen said with a smile, then turned to meet the next one who wanted a seat in the car.

Except for a couple of weddings, Jack hadn't been inside a church in close to fifteen years. It wasn't easy to find time when on duty at various forts. And once deployed, there'd been even less time. Maybe it was time to change that.

* * *

Allie opened the door to her car two hours later and felt the heat that had built up inside. She'd leave it open until they were ready to leave.

"So did you enjoy it?" she asked Jack. She hoped he had. Once or twice she'd been afraid he'd been overwhelmed. Everyone was so friendly, stopping to chat, to be introduced. But then she knew everyone. How would a stranger fare meeting almost half the town all in one day?

"I did."

She smiled. She hadn't been around Jack much, but she'd

already caught on to the fact he wasn't a talker.

"Good. Now you know some people, it'll be easier to go places in Rocky Point."

"Just because I've been exposed, doesn't mean I actually know anyone," he said as he got into the car.

"It's a first step. And they know you now, so they'll say hi when they see you." She climbed in, massaging her hip a little. It ached. She'd been on her feet too much. But the tour had been fascinating. She was so happy for Josh having found something he loved. He talked about racing in his future. Maybe another Grand Prix winner, she thought.

"You okay?" he asked.

She wrinkled her nose. Trust him to notice her discomfort. It took one to know one. "I will be, how are you holding up? Two gimps trying to do too much."

He smiled. Allie caught her breath. It was the first time she remembered him smiling. He was gorgeous. The scars on his face gave him an interesting look. There was a dimple on his left cheek that had her mesmerized. His eyes looked happy for the first time.

"Not very politically correct, are you? Everyone else dances around the issue," he said.

"Why? I won't ever walk like a normal person. You're limping more now than when we started out. I call it as I see it."

His smile faded. "Doesn't it bother you?"

"It did," she said, starting the engine and turning on the air conditioning. "But I've had years to get used to the situation. I prayed a lot about it, especially at first. I don't understand why I wasn't killed. I don't understand why I was left with a permanent limp and a constant ache that gets worse if I do too much. But I do understand I have my life, my health and my mind intact. Maybe my path is to help others with similar injuries who need encouragement. I love visiting the VA hospital. I only wish everyone was as fortunate as you and will walk out of there one day."

"You're a half full kind of gal, right?" he asked, eyes narrowed.

She nodded, watching for the pedestrians in the lot as she slowly backed out of the space. "I'm grateful for all I have. Sometimes I mourn what I lost, but mostly I try to be appreciative that I can walk at all, that I still have abilities to help others."

"Plus you have a good career."

"Right. But it wasn't my first choice of career," she said, as they left the lot behind and headed back toward Rocky Point.

"What was?"

"I was going to be a nurse. Join Doctors Without Borders and help those less fortunate than Americans."

"The crash ended that," he said slowly.

"Sure. I can hardly stand on my feet all day. I couldn't carry trays with one hand gripping a cane. So that dream ended. I found something else I like. But I'm never going around the world to help those less fortunate."

"Maybe your going to the VA is what you're supposed to do. You bring a lot to the men there, you know. Your visits give them a bright spot in an otherwise routine existence."

"I enjoy visiting with them. What's that?" Allie slammed on the brakes and pulled to the shoulder of the road. Before Jack could even guess what she was talking about, she was out of the car and dashing across the road, cane left behind.

Jack got out quickly, went around the car and shut her door so another car driving by wouldn't hit it. Then he looked for her. She was kneeling beside what looked like some kind of animal, crooning over it.

"Oh, you poor thing. Look at you, what happened?"

He crossed the road and stopped next to her. "It's a dog."

"Yes, and hurt, I think. Poor baby. We'll get you to a vet." She looked up at him. "If I pull the car closer over here, do you think that between the two of us we can get him into the back? I have some blankets there. We can take him to the vet's in Pineville. I think he was hit by a car. How could they not stop?"

Jack looked at the dog. It wasn't any breed he recognized. But then he didn't know breeds much beyond German Shepherds and Labs. It was a medium size dog—not a problem a year ago. Now his right arm was almost useless and he wasn't sure he could pick the dog up one handed, but maybe the two of them together could manage. Or flag down another car and get help.

Her look of entreaty was more than he could stand. "Sure, we'll manage somehow."

She smiled and petted the dog again. "Wait here, we'll bring the car close to you. But I won't run into you, don't be afraid."

She looked up again. "I forgot my cane. I can't get up. Can you help me?"

Jack reached out his left hand, took hers into his and easily pulled her to her feet. She didn't seem to weigh much.

She tucked her hand in against his elbow. "I need help back to the car. I can't believe I got all the way here without falling."

"Gimps have to stay together," he said, slowly walking back to the car.

She laughed, squeezing his arm. "You're funny. Thanks for helping."

It took more time than either expected, but they were able to get the dog into the back of the SUV. He lay quietly, watching them. Jack was just glad he hadn't bitten either of them.

When they reached the vet's, two of the vet techs took the dog in. Allie and Jack went to wait in the reception area until a vet tech came out. "Dr. Morris said you can come back and see the dog."

When they reached the small exam room, they found the dog on a stainless steel table, the doctor still examining him. Allie made introductions, then went to pat the dog. "Is he going to be all right?"

"Picked up another stray, eh?" the vet said, his hand gently assessing the dog.

"He was lying by the side of the road. Was he hit by a car?"

"Looks like it. I think his left hind leg is broken. We'll take x-rays and see what's up. Then I'll do what I can. Any idea who the owner is?"

She shook her head, still petting the dog.

"We checked for a microchip. None. With no collar or tags, we have to wait for someone to call in a lost dog. He's not a dog I recognize. I'll ask Tate--he's used to the routine; that's what happened with Faith's dog. She was a stray and when Faith found the owner, he no longer wanted her."

"There're better ways to relinquish a dog, than leave him by the side of the road or just turn him loose," Allie muttered.

"Some people just don't get it," the vet said. He finished and looked at her. "I'll call you later to let you know how he's doing."

"Okay." She looked at the vet. "And if no one claims him?"

"Guess you'll want to take him," the vet said with a smile.

"I could until I find him a home." He was a pretty dog with reddish brown fur and splashes of white around his neck and face, though his coat was matted and dirty.

"Do you know what kind of dog it is?" Jack asked.

"Mutt, I'd guess, but with a strong Border collie in him. He's a nice dog. I know he's in pain but he's not aggressive at all. We'll clean him up a bit and get that leg taken care of. I appreciate your good intentions, Allie, but if his leg's in a cast it might be hard for him to use stairs."

Allie bit her lip in indecision. "I guess I could ask my folks if they'd foster him, just until I find him a home or he can manage the steps."

"No need to decide right now. Who knows, the owner could be calling frantically around right now."

"But you don't think so," she said.

"He's undernourished, like he's been on his own for a while and isn't getting enough to eat."

"Summer people leaving a pet behind?" she asked.

"Or someone whose house was foreclosed and can't keep him anymore. I'll call you later and let you know how he's doing. If he does okay tonight and tomorrow, he'll be able to leave on Monday."

She nodded. "See you later, doggie," she said, turning to look at Jack. "I'm ready to leave if you are."

When they were back in the car heading for Jack's place, he said, "Do you do this kind of thing often?"

"Rescue strays? Yep, if I see them. If we don't take care of critters when they need help, who will?"

When they reached his home, she pulled into the driveway and looked at the house. "Too bad you have stairs, too, or the dog could stay with you."

"Whoa. I've never had a dog, I haven't a clue how to take care of one."

Still studying his front porch, she acted as if she hadn't heard him. "You only have two steps, and they are wide and shallow. I bet we could build a ramp and the dog could walk up that. My steps are too steep; it would be like trying to climb up a slide. But your place would be perfect."

"No."

She looked at him in startled surprise. "You don't want to help a poor defenseless dog? I'd think you two would bond——both being injured."

"Get real. I can hardly take care of myself, much less a dog."

"He wouldn't be any trouble. I could come over every day and feed him, brush him. Make sure he's not a bother. Your place would be perfect."

"What's wrong with your parents taking care of him, as you said before?" he asked.

"The thing is, they don't like me being out on my own. Any little thing gives them more ammunition to ambush me with time and again."

"Why?"

"They want me to move back home. Sometimes I think my mom is stuck in a time warp at the week after the accident. It was a bad time. I want to forget and move on. She can't get over her precious baby not being whole. I love her to bits, but she needs to stop smothering me."

Jack opened his door. "You'll find someone else," he said. He got out and closed it. He walked around to the driver's door. When she rolled down the window, he put his hand on the door. "Thanks for the outing."

"Want to go to church with me tomorrow?" she asked.

He shook his head. "Too much for one weekend. Maybe another time."

Allie watched him walk to the porch, take the shallow steps slowly. She still thought his taking care of the dog would be perfect. It would give him companionship and give the dog a nice place to recuperate. Neither would be up for strenuous walks or play—at least until the dog's leg healed.

She backed out of the drive in deep thought. Maybe the dog's owners would claim him. But she doubted it.

There had to be a way for her to find him a place to stay without involving her mom and dad.

* * *

Sunday morning, Allie entered the young adult Bible study classroom, greeted her friends and sat down beside Rachel. They'd been friends for years. Both still single, they often went out to dinner together or to a movie. Rachel ran her own business, too, an antique store on Main Street.

"Did you go to the track's open house yesterday?" she asked Allie. It was still several minutes before class would start.

"I did. Zack's doing a wonderful thing. The kids were so cute--devoted, knowledgeable, gaining self-confidence by the second. What a blessing."

"I wanted to go, but didn't have anyone to watch the shop. Glad now I stayed. I sold a couple of pieces. Did you go with Josh and his mother?"

"No, actually I took the newest resident of Rocky Point: Jack Donner."

"Do tell. Who is he?"

Allie quickly filled her in, ending with the situation with the dog.

"Would you want to foster him until his leg heals?" she asked her friend.

"You forget I have a puppy. Rocky would be too wild for

a dog supposed to be kept quiet while his leg heals."

"Yeah, I guess you're right. I tried to get Jack to do it, but he said no."

"A lot to ask of a stranger," Rachel said with a teasing grin. "Or is he more than a stranger?"

"Well, technically, you could say I've known of him for longer than I've known him. I never spoke to him at the VA hospital, but I saw him there. He seems so alone. I wish I could do something to bring him into the activities around here and help him make loads of friends. He seems lost somehow. Which is probably not true at all."

Allie knew people had to make their own friends. But some were more reticent than others, and she suspected Jack was more conscious of his injuries than he let on. She remembered how self-conscious she'd been when she'd first come home from the hospital. The awful feeling that everyone had been staring at her, assessing how much she could do and how handicapped she was. Now she accepted herself as she was and thanked God daily for all the abilities she still had.

Making her way to the sanctuary before the morning services, she was stopped by Tricia.

"I have your pictures," the girl said excitedly. "I think they came out great. Tell me the truth, however. What do you think?"

Allie slid the sheets from the large envelope and studied the three pictures of her in various poses in the racing car. "You did a good job. The lighting's good, the composition is balanced and you even managed to make it look like an action shot. Nicely done."

Tricia beamed. "Thanks. I'm applying all the techniques you've taught me."

"Yes, I see that."

Tricia looked around, "Did your friend come today?"

"Jack? Not today."

Tricia handed her another envelope. "He wanted copies of your pictures, too. So these are for him."

Allie took the second envelope, surprised to hear Jack had wanted copies. "I'll see he gets them," she said. Moving into the sanctuary, she spotted her parents and went to sit beside them.

"Hello, Honey." Her dad gave her a hug. Then her mother.

"Are you coming to lunch today?" she asked.

"Sure am."

"I have a pot roast in the slow cooker. Should be ready by one," her mother said with a smile.

Allie and her parents usually met for lunch after church. It was their main meal of the day on Sundays and she liked her mother's cooking better than her own. Plus she would rarely make a huge meal for one. If they didn't meet for lunch for some reason, Allie liked to treat herself at Marcie's café.

The service was about the Good Samaritan. Her mother glanced at her and murmured, "You know all about this one. You are always doing good for someone."

Allie nodded. She tried. From those to whom much had been given, much was expected. And she felt she'd been given so much. She could have died with Jason and the others in the van. Sometimes she caught herself thinking she'd see them around the next corner. It was hard to let go of friends she'd known all her life, shared birthday parties with, gone swimming with in summer and skiing in winter.

Shaking off the memories, she focused on the sermon. Then found her mind drifting again to Jack. She would take him the pictures later. She looked forward to seeing him again. Maybe he'd invite her to stay a little while.

Which would give her more time to convince him to take the dog if the owners didn't claim him. Maybe she'd push just a little bit to get him to consider it. Not commit, at least not yet. But just consider it.

* * *

It was mid-afternoon when Allie turned into the driveway of Jack's house. He was not on the porch. She hoped he hadn't gone somewhere. Carefully she picked up the quarter cut of devil's food cake her mother had made. When she'd learned of Jack, she'd insisted Allie take him a huge piece that he could enjoy over the next couple of days.

She reached the front door: still no Jack. If he had a dog, he would have had a warning that someone was here. The old house didn't have a door bell. She knocked. Waiting a couple of minutes, she tried again. Finally banging on it so he'd hear. She knew he'd lost part of his hearing in the IED attack.

The door opened and he stood there, looking sleep-warm and rumpled. Her heart kicked into high gear. His eyes studied her and she stood mesmerized in his gaze. The deep blue rivaled that of the sea on a sunny day. His hair was a bit mussed and she longed to smooth it back.

"Oh, did I wake you up?" She hadn't thought he'd be asleep. It was the middle of the afternoon.

"Guess I fell asleep," he mumbled. "Did I know you were coming?"

"How could you? I didn't know myself until after church. Can I come in?"

"If that cake's for me, you sure can."

She smiled. "This is from my mom. She believes in the power of chocolate."

"The power of chocolate?" He stepped aside so she could enter.

"To make any day brighter. I'm entirely in agreement." Allie noted the floor plan as she walked to the back where she expected the kitchen would be. The living room gave way to the dining room and at the back was the kitchen. She placed the cake dish on the counter and turned, holding out the envelope.

"Tricia said you wanted these."

Jack opened the envelope, sliding out the three photographs. The teenager had done a great job capturing Allie's bubbling enchantment with the race car. With the entire day. He wanted to smile back at the picture.

"Yeah, thanks."

Allie went to look out the window over the sink. The back yard was flat with a few large stones sticking up. The lawn was brown but cut. Not too far away was a line of trees, bent from the ocean breezes.

"It's nice and flat here and the doggie would be able to walk around to do his business," she murmured.

"Are you talking?" Jack asked, putting the pictures on the counter and looking at Allie.

She'd forgotten he couldn't hear well. So much for being subtle. She faced him. "I said this would be a good yard for a dog."

He broke into a smile. "That again?"

"Or still. The vet called this morning and said he was doing well."

"The vet?"

"The dog. And he could be picked up tomorrow. We should give him a name."

"We should let the authorities take care of the dog."

Allie frowned, this was not going like she hoped. "Well, pray about it."

"Pray about it?" he repeated.

She nodded. "Don't you take things to the Lord so He can work them out?"

"No." He thought a moment. "Maybe when under fire or infiltrating an enemy-held town."

That surprised her. "I talk to the Lord all the time. I couldn't make it through the day without His help. You should pray about taking the dog. At least temporarily. Plus, walking around town with a dog will get everyone to stop and talk to you."

"Really?"

"Oh, yes. Dogs are people magnets. I dare you to walk down the length of Main Street with one and not talk to half a dozen people at least. Especially with a story to tell about why his leg's in a cast."

Jack considered what she said. He'd returned home yesterday tired but satisfied. He'd met so many people, he'd never remember them all. But they'd probably remember him. It was a step. If he planned to remain in Rocky Point, what she suggested might have some merit. He looked beyond her, out the window. That was the question. Did he want to remain? Become a part of the community? He hadn't a clue how to do that. He'd led a nomadic life since his mother died. Was he capable of change?

Allie watched him. She could almost see the idea taking root. Nearly holding her breath, she wondered if she should say more to push it along, or wait and let him come to his own conclusion that her idea was brilliant.

When Jack looked at her she almost shouted in jubilation. She knew he was going to say yes.

"On the condition you come and help take care of him," he said.

She smiled. "Deal."

The dog would have a home, and she'd have an excuse to visit Jack Donner every day.

Chapter Three

Monday morning, Allie checked her calendar for her schedule. The major event this week for her would be taking pictures at George Watson's birthday party at the church. George lived with his granddaughter and her family, and was active in the Senior Center and senior activities at Trinity. Allie couldn't help smiling when she thought about George. No one ever thought he'd slow down. She hoped she'd be as active and sharp as he was if she reached her nineties.

She should invite Jack. He was Army, George was Army. They would have something to talk about.

Would he attend? She'd never know unless she asked.

The phone rang. It was Rachel on the other end.

"What's up?" Allie said. Rachel was probably home. She closed her shop on Sundays and Mondays.

"I think I need a new ad and want a picture of this lovely armoire I got from an estate sale last week."

"Sure. Shall I come by today?"

"That would be great, no customers to interrupt. What time?"

"I need to check on the dog first."

"You taking it?" Rachel asked.

"No, Jack is."

"Wow, how did you swing that?"

"I'll tell you all about it when I get there. Let's meet around ten. Does that work for you?"

"Sure. I can't wait to hear more about Jack."

"You mean his taking the dog."

"Whatever you say. See you then."

Allie verified with the vet she could pick up the dog in the afternoon. She called Jack to see if he wanted to ride over with her.

"I think you can manage by yourself," he said. "He will be mobile, won't he?"

"Sure, but it would be nice for the dog to see both of us, don't you think? He can get used to you on the ride home."

"He's coming to visit, not stay the rest of his life."

She laughed. She had hoped for a bit more enthusiasm, but she wasn't giving up.

"We'll stop at the store before we pick him up to get some things. You can meet more people." What would be the trigger to get him to agree?

"What does a dog need? Some food, right?"

"Food, yes, but also a doggie bed, a leash and collar. Maybe a few toys."

Jack was silent for a long moment. "Remind me about this being temporary."

"He'll need some things and he can take them with him when he moves in with me," she said, laughing. Did he see right through her—her hope that he would love this dog and have a constant companion?

"And we could do lunch at Marcie's," she suggested.

"I'll pass."

"I'll be there at one, then." She hung up wondering if he would ever consider going to the birthday party. He was a hard sell for a mere ride to the vet's. He confused her. He'd moved to town, yet seemed very reluctant to become involved in anything. He didn't strike her as a shy man. He was strong, confident and assured.

And good looking to boot, despite the scars on his face.

It had to be part of the recovery process. She tried to remember back when she first came home. There'd been days of depression, sadness, anger. Her entire life had changed. So had Jack's.

"Cut him some slack, girl," she said, as she went to get dressed for the day. "You more than anyone else around here know what he's going through."

Which made her just the one to save the soldier from himself—introduce him around town, give him a sense of belonging.

She had a job and a doggie to get settled. She wanted Jack to stay. Already feeling a special bond with him, she didn't like the thought he'd move on. She hoped he'd find a job and settle in Rocky Point.

Settle near her? Maybe even see her as more than a friend?

She frowned, driving the thought away. They could be friends. That's all.

* * *

Promptly at ten, she arrived at the antique shop Rachel owned on Main Street. It was about halfway between the marina at the end of the street and Marcie's café at the top. The large windows displayed two pieces of Victorian furniture in one and a collection of hat pins and fancy hat in the other. Rachel rotated the displays every two weeks. Her business was slow during the winter months, but there were still sales to be made.

"Hi, right on time," Rachel said giving her a hug. She quickly closed and locked the door behind Allie. "Don't want anyone to think I'm open today. This way we'll work undisturbed. Come on, the armoire is in the back."

Allie followed her to the storage area. While the front part of the shop had elegant displays, the back was crowded with furniture, memorabilia from bygone days, and even some vintage clothing that was sought out by the little local theater group.

"So tell me about this Jack," Rachel said, as she stopped beside a lovely cherry wood armoire.

"He said he'd foster the dog until the cast comes off."

"Not that. What's he like. We hardly had a chance to talk yesterday in church. What does he look like?"

Allie smiled. "When he smiles he's amazingly handsome. But mostly he looks serious and mad."

"That tells me nothing."

"Okay, he's tall, I'd say over six feet, but I'm not sure exactly how tall. He has dark hair and blue eyes like the sea. His hair is cut short--he's ex-military."

"Ah, a soldier?"

"Yep, Army. That's what got him so injured he won't be going back. I don't know all that happened. He's not really talkative. He walks with a limp, he's deaf in one ear and there are scars I can see on the right side--so I figure he was hurt only on the one side. But I forget about that when I'm around him. He just looks so fit. Broad shoulders, muscular chest. And strong--except for his right arm. That still needs to gain strength."

Rachel leaned against one of the antique oak tables nearby and watched Allie talk.

"You like him," she said, when her friend wound down.

"Of course I like him. He's likable."

"Doesn't sound so much like it if he's mad all the time."

"Not with people, with circumstances. From the little he's said, I think he loved being in the Army. Some people really like that lifestyle," Allie defended.

"Not the war zones, I bet."

"Well, probably not that. Sometimes he reminds me of a kid who doesn't know what to do. Other times, he can be stubborn."

"How much time have you spent with him?"

Allie realized not a lot of time if measured in minutes and hours. How had she picked up on so much? Or was she attributing characteristics where they weren't? No. She felt an affinity with Jack she had never felt with another.

"Not much. I think it's that we've shared similar devastating experiences."

"So you've found someone who can really relate to what happened to you," Rachel said slowly.

"Maybe. But we don't talk about it, at least not beyond the basics of what happened." She unpacked her camera and attached the duel flashes. "So what are you looking for in your ad?"

"Show this to its best advantage. Crop out the other stuff around it. I thought we could do a closed shot to show the carving and maybe one with the doors open. It's such a great find. It looks almost as new as the day it was made, which I calculate to be around 1850."

"Let's see what I can do," Allie said, glad to have moved off the topic of Jack.

She enjoyed the variety of her work and took numerous photographs from all different angles. The lighting was adjusted for maximum benefit.

"Okay, I'll print these out and bring them by later. You going to be here or at home?"

"When do you think that'll be?"

"After our trip to the vet this afternoon."

"Ah, will you have the mysterious Jack Donner with you?"

"He's not mysterious," Allie protested with a laugh. "And sure, I can stop by on our way home from the vet. You'll like him, I bet."

Rachel closed the armoire and glanced at Allie. "The question I'm more concerned with is how much you like him."

Allie had a lot of friends. She'd grown up in Rocky

Point, attended the local schools and church. She was still friends with kids she'd gone to high school with. Though her two special friends had died in the van crash.

She'd only known Jack a very short time, yet she couldn't deny he felt special too. How and why, she wasn't ready to delve into.

"He's a friend. Don't go playing matchmaker on me," Allie said, packing her camera back in its case.

"Oooh, matchmaker. I was just asking about him being a friend. What gives?"

"Nothing. If something develops, you'll be the first to know."

"Spoken like a true photographer. I look forward to meeting him."

Allie drove home flustered that Rachel was reading more into her comments about Jack than they warranted. But she couldn't deny how excited she was to see him again in only a few hours.

*   *   *

Jack was getting used to waiting for Allie's arrival from his spot on the porch. He liked the fresh air and slight tang of salt in the breeze from the ocean. The weather continued mild, and he hoped he'd be up to Maine winters when the cold and snow came. Did the town clear the road all the way to his house? Maybe he should have questioned that before renting the place.

Allie's SUV came into view and he walked to the drive so

she didn't have to get out.

"Hi." Her bright smile was all he needed to feel optimistic about life in general. If she could bottle that, she'd make a mint selling it to the world.

"I have a car. Want to go in that?" he asked.

"Not unless it's big like this one. I think the dog will do better in the cargo area than on one of the seats."

Since his was a sedan, he nodded and climbed in.

The first stop was the local hardware store. To his surprise, there was a pet section.

"Tate's dad owns the shop, and since Faith has a dog now, he started carrying some bare necessities," Allie explained as she led the way to the back where two shelves carried pet items.

Since there were three different kinds of dog beds, an assortment of dog crates and an entire rack of toys, collars and leashes, he thought the man had gone beyond bare necessities.

"Tate's the Sheriff, right?" He was trying to keep people straight.

"Right, and Faith's his fiancee. She's the nurse at the clinic."

"Okay, I met her."

Allie picked out things, handing them to Jack to hold. For a moment he was bemused. He couldn't ever remember shopping with anyone since he'd started buying his own clothes at age thirteen. Allie looked like a woman on a mission. She discussed the color of the collar–like the dog would care, or even see it. She debated on the leash, the dog dish and water dish. When it came to the bed, she asked which he thought would do best. She took a chew toy and a couple of balls, balancing them in one hand while her other clutched her cane. Both of them were balancing things when they went to the register.

A young man greeted Allie and she introduced him to Jack as Ethan Potter.

"And we need a bed for a dog. He's about fifty pounds, the vet said. How big a bed do we need?"

"Any particular kind in mind?"

She shook her head. "I haven't a clue."

"Then I'll get you a big one, so the dog can stretch out if he wants, or curl up."

Ethan was back in a couple of minutes with a large square cushion that would serve as a bed for the dog.

Jack looked at all the things Ethan was ringing up. It looked like a lot for a dog staying only a few weeks until the cast came off.

"What about food?" he asked, noting its absence.

"I wanted to see what the vet said about that," Allie replied. "Then we can stop at the grocery store and get whatever brand of food he recommends. Oh, and I have another stop; it'll be quick."

"Where?" Jack asked.

"I did some work this morning, and want to show the preliminary proofs to my client so I can work on it later this evening. It's at the antique store on Main Street. My friend Rachel owns it. And she'll want to see our dog, too. I thought about her first to foster our dog, but she has a puppy, and it wouldn't be good for recuperating to have a wild puppy around."

Jack heard the *our dog*. It had a nice ring. Something in common, something shared.

* * *

When they arrived at the veterinary office, the vet tech took them right into one of the exam rooms. In only a moment she led in the dog.

"Wow, he's so pretty now that he's cleaned up!" Allie exclaimed, as she leaned over to pet him. He wagged his tail so hard, he lost his balance with the cast and sat down. The surprised look on his face had her laugh aloud.

Jack acknowledged the bath had done a lot for the dog, but his focus was on Allie. He smiled in reaction to her delight. She found such joy in the most mundane things. Which was one reason he liked being around her. She brightened the entire day—most of which could always use brightening.

"How's he doing?"

"Seems to be okay. Dr. Morris will be in soon to give you an update." The girl handed Allie the leash, petted the dog again and left.

"Hi, Doggie. You look so pretty all cleaned up. Look, Jack, at how white his fur is now that there's no mud on it."

She sat on the bench along one wall and the dog half limped half ran over to her, skidding to a stop and sitting abruptly. "Oh, you are a beauty, aren't you?"

When Allie looked up at Jack, he almost caught his

breath at how pretty she was when her entire face lit up with happiness.

"He looks better." He wasn't one to gush over a dog. He had to admit the little guy looked much more appealing now that he was cleaned up, with no tangles and burrs or mud marring his coat.

Dr. Morris entered. "What do you think of our fellow now?"

"He's beautiful," Allie said.

"He did clean up well. And is getting around with the cast, though sometimes he falls over. But he'll get used to it. We put out the word about him to local agencies. I've given him all the vaccines he should have, just to be safe. His last pain pill was given early this morning, and you can see it's worn off. He was more lethargic earlier. You need to keep him as quiet as possible—especially these first few days. We want that bone to set perfectly."

"So you'll let us know if his owners contact you?" Allie said.

"Absolutely. But I suspect he was abandoned. He's been eating like there's no tomorrow."

They discussed diet, restrictions and other aspects of his care. Allie put his new collar on and snapped on the new leather leash they'd bought. Then Allie handed Jack the leash.

"I don't want him to pull me off balance. He's never going to pull you over," she explained.

Jack took it and looked at the dog. He'd wanted a pet when he'd been a kid. But that'd been years ago. He wasn't sure this was a good idea. But he had committed to taking him and he lived by his word.

"So you have a way to get him into the car and out? I do not want him jumping out. That could undo all the work I've done," Dr. Morris said.

"There's some lumber at the house. We could make a kind of ramp for him to get down from the car. Can you or your staff get him in?" Jack asked. He'd thought about that himself. The SUV was higher than his own car, and it wouldn't be easy for a dog to get out of. Neither one of them could lift the dog out. He'd have to come up with a way.

Once the three of them were in the car, Allie turned around. The dog rested his head on the back of the seat, looking at them from the cargo area.

"You stay there, don't be jumping into the back seat," she said.

Jack turned, and they could tell by his movements the dog was wagging his tail.

"I want you to meet my friend Rachel, but maybe you better stay in the car with the dog so he won't get lonely," she said as they began the drive home.

"He'll be fine for a few minutes. That's as long as you plan to be, right?" Jack said. Any other time he'd have been fine with staying in the car, but he was curious about Allie's friend. He knew the men at the VA loved Allie's visits. He'd seen her popularity at the open house at the track. Now he could see someone else who'd know her for years. A person could learn a lot about someone by their friends.

Allie found a parking place only two doors away from

the antique shop. The day was sunny and breezy. She rolled down the windows. "Do you think he'll try to get out of the car with the windows down?" she asked, looking back at the dog.

"I don't know. Maybe I better stay with him." Jack would have to meet Rachel another time.

"I won't be long." She reached for the folder in the back seat and soon entered the antique shop.

Jack glanced around at the dog, who had his nose against the glass staring after Allie.

Jack massaged his shoulder. The ache never seemed to completely go away. It would with time, so the doctors had said. Maybe. Or maybe he'd just learn to live with it. He stared down the street. The ocean lay at the foot of Main Street. The old brick buildings lining the street looked solid. Many dated back two centuries. New Englanders built to last. His house was a case in point.

The dog whined. Jack looked over his shoulder. Allie and another woman were walking on the sidewalk heading for the car.

They came to the passenger door.

"Jack, this is my friend Rachel. Rachel, Jack Donner. And in the back is our dog."

"Hi Jack, nice to meet you." Rachel looked at the dog. "Oh, isn't he a pretty one—almost too pretty to be a boy dog. What's his name?"

Allie looked at Jack.

"Don't look at me, I don't know," he said.

"You have to name him. We can't just call him Doggie."

He shrugged. "Works for me."

"How would you like it if I called you Man?" she asked, exasperated.

He wouldn't care what she called him, as long as she hung around.

"Allie tells me you rented the Stafford place. How do you like Rocky Point?" Rachel asked.

"Nice town," he said. What he'd seen of it. If he planned to stay, he needed to put forth more effort to mingle with the town's citizens, get involved in something. The thought had him instantly longing for the house and its isolation. So maybe that was asking more than he could do right now. He'd take it slow. See what happened.

"I've been here since I was a teenager and came to live with my grandmother. She owned the shop before me. If you ever want to get some nice antique furnishings, stop by," Rachel said with a friendly smile.

He nodded, not sure he'd heard all she said.

"I'll give you the service man's discount." She grew serious. "Thank you for your service. We all appreciate it." She reached out and touched him lightly on the shoulder, as if she had to make contact.

Jack nodded again. He didn't need thanks. It had been his honor to serve in the military. He didn't know how to handle gratitude for doing what he'd loved.

"We'll take off now," Allie said. "Have to get the dog settled."

"Will we see you at George's party?" Rachel asked Jack, as Allie rounded the hood of the car.

"I didn't tell him about that yet," Allie called over the hood. "See you, Rachel."

"Do come. George would love to talk to another soldier," Rachel said. She smiled and gave a small wave when they pulled away.

"What was that about?" he asked as Allie drove back to his place.

"George Watson is one of the town heroes. He served in World War Two and in Korea. He was a military man like you—Army. He's in his nineties and celebrating another birthday this weekend. The church is putting on the party. You should come—Army men sticking together."

"We hardly have anything in common. And I'm no longer Army."

"Hmm, I heard once a Marine always a Marine. I thought that would be true of the Army, too."

He still felt Army. She was right, he always would, despite the injuries that kept him from returning to active duty.

"Come, if only to meet George. He'd love to talk to another soldier. And if you don't like it once you're there, you can leave right away."

"How many people will be there?" Jack asked. He wasn't up to some large gathering. He knew he had to get over avoiding people, but it was hard to miss out on conversations because of his hearing loss. Trying to keep up made him feel particularly awkward.

She glanced at him. He knew before she spoke what she'd say.

"Lots. It's a big deal to celebrate George's birthday. But I promise you won't have to stay if you don't like it."

"Where?" He could feel himself wavering. Maybe it'd be good to talk to a soldier who no longer served. Of course they'd have nothing in common--the age difference alone made that a fact. He was finding it harder and harder to refuse Allie's requests.

"At the church fellowship hall. It starts at one o'clock. I could come by and pick you up."

"I can drive," he said. And that way he could leave when he wanted.

"So you'll come?" she asked brightly.

"I'll think about it." Jack had no idea moving to Rocky Point would get him tangled up with Allie. He'd merely hoped to find a quiet place to live, one that sounded like a fairy tale setting to a boy from the Midwest who had no family and no good memories of growing up.

A quick stop at the grocery store produced the dog's food and a box of biscuits.

When they reached Jack's place, he had Allie keep the doors closed while he went to drag out the wide plank he'd spoken of at the vet's office, and together they flanked the dog and made him walk down the ramp, rather than hop out which is what Jack thought the dog wanted to do.

"Be good for Jack, now," Allie admonished. She reached in for the bag from the hardware store. "I can't manage the bed, can you?" she asked.

He nodded, holding the leash as the dog sniffed in an ever widening circle, until the leash kept him from moving farther.

"Take him by some bushes. Dogs like that," she said.

"Did you have a dog as a kid?" he asked.

"Of course. Our last one died just over a year ago. My folks say they won't get another, but I saw Mom with Faith's dog when she was still nursing her puppies and I think they'll change their mind soon. They needed to grieve our old dog before getting another one."

The dog soon finished his business and Jack placed the wide plank on the steps, guiding the dog up. Once in the house, he took off the leash and watched a moment. The dog sniffed around the furniture, along the floor and wound up in the kitchen, where Allie placed the bag of dog food.

"Call me later to let me know how things are going," she said. "Do you need directions to the church?"

"Are you not planning to be over before then?" Jack asked. "I thought we were in this dog fostering gig together."

"Sure, but I expect he won't be a bit of trouble." She picked up the tennis balls they'd bought, opened the canister and tossed the ball toward the dog. He lunged for it, catching it in his mouth.

"Oh, doggie, good catch! My bad, however. I should not have thrown it at him and made him lunge like that."

The dog came over to Allie and laid the ball at her feet, retreating a dozen feet and looking at her with anticipation.

"Now you've started something," Jack said. He leaned over and picked up the ball, tossing it gently so it landed right in the dog's mouth without him having to move.

Wagging his tail, the dog came to lay the ball at Jack's feet and retreated once more, turning to face him.

"You two will have hours of fun with that," Allie said. "Call me."

Jack reached out and caught her arm, stopping her.

She looked up expectantly.

He couldn't say a word. Just looked at her. Her expression became quizzical. Her skin beneath his hand was soft and warm. Her eyes were dancing as they stared back into his. He had the strongest urge to lean over and kiss her. To touch her mouth with his, envelop her in his arms and never let go.

"Nothing. I'll call you later and tell you how the dog's doing." It was an effort to release her. He did it and took a step back, wishing she'd step nearer.

"Think up a name for him," she said with a grin.

Allie didn't want to leave. For a long moment she'd thought he was going to kiss her! His eyes had gazed into hers with an expression she couldn't decipher. It would have been so easy to step closer, raise her face for a kiss.

Then he'd stepped back and she knew she'd misread the situation. She had work to do, and wanted to get Rachel's feedback so she could finalize the images she chose. Almost running away from the kitchen, she felt a wash of embarrassment. She hoped he didn't read minds.

As she backed out of the driveway, however, she glanced wistfully at the old house. She wished he'd asked her to stay longer.

And that he had kissed her.

* * *

The entire time she worked on the pictures Rachel had selected, Allie kept her ear tuned for the phone. He would call, wouldn't he? She wanted to know how the dog was doing.

And talk to Jack.

She was starting dinner when the phone rang.

"Hello?"

"Your dog is tireless," he said without a greeting.

"My dog! If anything, he's our dog. What do you mean tireless? You're not letting him be too active are you? He's supposed to be resting while his leg heals."

"I'll hand him the phone and you explain that to him. We played ball for a while, then when I sat down, he jumped up on the couch."

"He's not supposed--"

"Hey, I know what he's supposed to do and not do, but he didn't get the message. Anyway, I took him out a couple of times. At least he knows how to do his business. And he ate dinner a few minutes ago, then brought me the ball."

Allie giggled. "He obviously loves to play catch."

"Yeah, and he's good at it. As long as I lob it right to his face he can catch it without moving. Only sometimes it bounces off him and then he goes tearing after it. The cast on his leg doesn't seem to bother him too much."

"So why are you calling?"

"I don't have the vet's number and I want to make sure he's going to be okay with this activity."

"You could take the ball away from him and not throw it," she suggested.

The silence went on for a few seconds. "You come do

that. He looks too sad when I do."

She laughed again. "Who would have expected the big brave soldier would be ruled by a little dog."

"Hey, I'm not ruled by him. But he's injured. He needs special attention."

Allie thought about Jack. He, too, was injured, not only physically, but in his heart. She wished she could help him like he was helping the dog.

"I'll call the vet and see what he says. And if he says no ball, then you have to take it away from him. It's not always easy being the one in charge."

"Let me know." He gave her his phone number and hung up.

Allie called the vet's and got the after-hours answering service. She told the woman on the phone her concerns and she promised to have the vet call Allie back.

Not wanting to take the time to cook something, Allie prepared a salad and toasted some rye bread for dinner. She had almost finished when Dr. Morris called. When she explained, he said in this case, the dog probably knew what he could do or not do. If he was not in any obvious pain, the cast was probably holding the limb immobile. He told her to try to keep him from jumping or spending too much time on the injured leg.

Which was what the vet had said at the hospital when they picked up the dog.

She grabbed her keys and headed for Jack's place. She'd see for herself what the dog was up to.

When she arrived, it was dusk. The sun had set, the sea

already dark. She heard the weirdest yelp-yodel sound from the house. Before she reached the porch, Jack opened the front door and the dog tore out, half running half lurching to get to Allie.

"Well, hello, what a nice welcome," she said, leaning over to pet the dog. His back end wagged so much he almost toppled over.

"You think something happened to his voice? That was the oddest bark I ever heard," Jack said from the doorway.

"I don't know. I don't think he was injured there; the vet would have mentioned other injuries. I talked to him."

"Come in." Jack invited, holding the door wide.

When Allie was seated on the old sofa, the dog jumped right up beside her and laid his head in her lap, gazing up at her as if she were the best thing he'd ever seen.

"What a precious dog you are!" she exclaimed, petting his soft fur.

"What a suck up, you mean." Jack sat at the other end of the sofa, looking at the two of them. "He was my best pal until you showed up."

"Sorry," she said with a grin.

"Naw, it shows he has good taste."

She glanced away at the backhanded compliment and quickly related what the vet had said.

"So he seems quiet enough now," she said softly, still running her hands over his soft fur. He closed his eyes and, in only a few minutes, she knew he was asleep.

"Try getting up. Or wait a few minutes, he'll jump up and go get his ball."

"He seems to be settling in well enough. Have you thought of a name for him?"

"No owners looking for him?"

"Not that I've heard," she replied.

Jack didn't respond, just watched as Allie petted the dog. They both looked quite content. While he felt a restlessness he hadn't felt in a long time.

"Want something to drink?" he asked.

The dog's head zapped up and he looked over his shoulder at Jack.

"You have a bowl of water; you can get your own drink whenever you want," Jack told him.

"I'm fine."

"I have some of that cake your mother sent over."

"No, thanks."

They lapsed into silence. Jack sought for something to say, anything to break the lengthening silence.

"He's asleep again," she said softly.

"Lucky dog that he can drop off in a heartbeat," Jack said. He couldn't envy a dog, but he wished his own nights brought sleep so quickly.

"You don't?" she asked.

"Not most nights."

"I'm going to the VA on Thursday this week. Want to go with me? See your friends there?" she said.

Jack thought about it for a moment. "I'll let you know." It depended on how he felt by Thursday. The weekend had been tough on him physically and he didn't want to get there and wimp out. He should be heeding the advice of the veteran's doctor--his own doctor--and rest up before doing more. But he was impatient with how long it was taking to get better.

Not that the VA doctor had held out much hope of him getting much better than he already was. He'd injured muscles and damaged joints. His hearing loss was permanent, and he might never have full range of motion on his right arm.

But it could improve. He knew that. The physical therapist had been more hopeful and given him a set of exercises designed to gain as much mobility and strength as possible. He did them faithfully every day, no matter how tired he was or how much pain he had.

He also threw the ball for the dog. When he started the ball just fell from his hand. Now he could lob it several feet.

Some of the guys there would never recover as much as. They'd all cheered when they'd heard he was being released. He wished he could be there when the rest of them got released.

"I usually leave around eleven, get a bite to eat when I reach Portland, and then arrive at the hospital around one and stay until three or so."

He knew her routine. Did she have any idea how much the men looked forward to her visits?

"Do we just leave the dog here?" he asked.

Allie looked at the sleeping animal. "I'll call there tomorrow and see if they'll let us bring him. I know therapy dogs have great results with patients. I bet your friends would like to see him. Let's see how he does over the next couple of days. If he has nice manners, I think he'd be a hit."

"Right, everyone's drawn to dogs."

"Mark my words, that's totally true," she replied with a wide smile. "But if we do take him, he better have a name. How can you introduce him properly with no name?"

* * *

Thursday morning, Allie swung by Jack's place to pick him and the dog up. She'd spoken with the director of the hospital and the man had been all for bringing the dog to the community room. Those who were able to spend the day there would love to see the dog, he said.

Jack brought the wooden ramp they used, getting the dog in the back of the SUV and then stowing it sideways along the side. Allie had put down the back seat, so the dog had the entire range of the car behind the front seats.

Jack had mixed emotions about going back to the hospital. He knew he'd be going there once in a while for checkups. But he'd only been gone a couple of weeks and was already heading back. The last couple of days he'd spent a lot of time outside with the dog, taking slow walks along the bluff, while the dog sniffed every blade of the sparsely growing grass and every rock scattered everywhere. Jack soon learned the dog didn't need a leash when they were around the house. He never wandered far from Jack. The weather had continued balmy during the day and cool at night. The forecast held for the next few days as well.

Time hung heavy on his hands. He wasn't used to so

much down time. And his inability to do what he was trained to do rubbed him raw. He wished there was something meaningful to fill the hours.

"Are you from New England?" Allie asked when they'd left Rocky Point behind.

"No. Raised in the Midwest."

"Do you have fall colors like these, then?" she said, sweeping her hand to indicate the brilliant colors of the trees lining the highway. The golds were bright in the sun, the reds appeared almost crimson. The yellows seemed to reflect the sunshine tenfold.

"Nothing like this."

"We have a tourists coming in to see the colors now. They'll be filling the hotel and bed and breakfasts until Thanksgiving. Then there a few diehards who like to come up to town during Christmas. We go all out in decorating Main Street."

He didn't go in for holiday decorating--never having had more than a small apartment. Sometimes on base, sometimes off base. And since he'd moved every few years, the less stuff he'd had the easier it was. He bet Allie was big on making a huge splash for every holiday.

"Did you pick out a name for the dog?" she asked.

He drew a deep breath. "I did." He glanced at her. Would she think him stupidly sentimental when she learned the name and why he picked it?

"Well, what?"

"Able."

"Abel? Like Cain and Abel?"

"No, like Able Company—the name of our company over in Afghanistan."

"Umm. Okay." She glanced at him. "To remember?"

He nodded. "To remember those who didn't make it home."

"Able," she tried it out.

The dog put his head on her shoulder.

"Wow, he knows it already. Good job, Able. You're a good dog."

The lick along her cheek caught her by surprise.

"Oh, yuck," she said, cringing away.

Jack laughed. "Forgot to tell you he licks sometimes."

"Next time warn me." She rubbed her cheek. "Doggie kisses are not something I relish." Then she grinned. "I remember one of the dogs we had was always licking everyone—it was especially sloppy just after she drank water and was still dripping."

It was easy to be with Allie, Jack realized as they sped down the highway. She could talk without expecting comments at every turn--or to have him come up with something to say. It was both restful and stimulating. He never knew where the topic would lead. Once she'd talked about her dog, she moved to other dogs, then high school athletics, both about when she was in school, and about the children involved today whom she photographed for class pictures and the local newspaper.

"You have an eclectic mix of photography jobs," he said at one point.

"Sure. There's not enough of any one thing in and

around Rocky Point, so I have to be available for all kinds of jobs."

"You ever think of moving to a bigger place? Portland or Boston?"

"No, not anymore."

"So you did once?"

"Don't all teenagers? I think everyone wants to leave the nest and set the world on fire. The ones who attempt it are lucky. You did, right? Going into the military?"

"I wanted to leave, but not set the world on fire. More to find a place for myself."

"What do you mean? You'll always have a place where you grew up, and sometimes that's the best place to be. Family and friends you've known all your life."

He nodded. "And sometimes it's not. I was raised in foster care. Nice enough people, but never a real family. The military became my family."

"Oh." She was silent for a moment. "Don't you keep in touch with your foster parents?"

"I had too many to keep in touch. I write at Christmas to one I really liked. But the husband lost his job and they couldn't afford to keep the apartment they had, so they got taken off the rolls." And he got sent to yet another home.

"Doesn't the military move everyone around all the time? I would think that's hard to keep friends."

"We move to different duty stations. But give it enough time and you're back with men and women you've served with before."

"Hmm, I guess. Not quite the same," she murmured.

"Let me guess, you had the picture perfect childhood, and when it came time to leave, you decided to stay where everyone loves you."

She glanced at him, her expression somber.

"Not exactly. I was going to leave. The crash changed everything."

Instantly he recalled her saying she'd planned to be a nurse and travel the globe, helping in third world countries that otherwise wouldn't have much medical care. They both had that in common: injured beyond repair and unable to pursue their dreams.

Not that those circumstances seemed to slow down Allie. She was full of life. Finding enchantment in so many things like—climbing down a dangerous cliff to capture the first rays of a sunrise. He'd walked near the cliff many times over the last couple of weeks and could vouch for how dangerous it looked. Or enjoying a meal at her friend's café, or talking about the delight she had in the open house they'd attended.

She'd showered the teenagers with compliments at the track's open house. And she'd jumped out of a car to save an unknown dog with no concern for her own safety. He didn't know how she could be so happy with the limitations life had thrown her way. But if there was a secret—he wanted it.

* * *

"I told you I got the okay to bring Able. But I didn't tell anyone you were coming. I thought it'd be a nice surprise," she said, when she turned into the parking lot of the VA hospital a couple of hours later.

"Just as well. I wasn't even sure myself until last night," Jack said. "Able, you wait until I get your ramp." The dog was already on his feet, tail and back end wagging furiously.

When they entered the visiting area a few moments later, the men seemed equally as glad to see him as they did Allie. And Able was a definite hit.

Jack was surprised at the feeling of homecoming he experienced. This was not a home, merely a way station while men tried to recover enough to leave. The fact some never would always stayed with him, but he refused to let those thoughts show.

"When did you get a dog, man?" Solly asked. His electric-powered wheelchair zoomed over to them. Without any prompting, the dog put his front legs on Solly's knees and wagged his tail. "Cool, man." Solly petted the dog with his good hand, a smile filling his face.

"Rescued him from the side of the road," Allie said, leaning over to give Solly a hug. "Jack's watching him until he gets better. Too many stairs at my house."

"What I want to know is how Jack wormed his way into your life, Allie," one of the men called. "I didn't even know you two knew each other."

"We didn't before he moved to Rocky Point. But now we do," she said, with a smile for Jack. How could she have missed him when she visited before? He seemed to dominate the room. Was it because he was standing, had some color in his face from his long walks in the sunshine? Or was it because she was attuned to him now?

There were several teasing comments thrown his way. He fielded them and finally admitted to checking out Rocky Point because of Allie's stories of the place.

"Is it as nice as she says?" Paul asked, leaning on his crutches. He'd come across the room to see the dog.

"So far, it lives up to its reputation."

"Jack needs to get involved more, then he could tell you a bunch of stories himself," Allie said, sitting in a chair someone pushed closer to her.

"Where're you living man?"

"How's the PT going?" another called.

"I never had a dog, how's that going?"

"What I want to know is how often you're seeing Allie?" Solly said, his eyes narrowed as he studied the two of them.

The questions came from everyone, but the last one caused them all to roar with laughter.

Jack glanced at Allie to see a faint hint of color on her face, though she was laughing with the rest of them. What would they all say if he responded that he wasn't seeing her enough?

"One thing at a time. We're here for a few hours."

The time seemed to fly by. Every last man in the place had a turn petting or sitting beside Able. The Border collie proved to be a huge hit and Jack thought the guys were sorrier to see Able leave, than they were to see Jack and Allie leave.

"Bring Able back next week," was the common theme as they left.

"That went well," Allie said when they were settled in the car. "Aren't you glad you came?"

"I am. There are some really great guys in there. It's a waste that they'll be forever handicapped. Some of them won't ever get out on their own."

"I know. We don't always understand God's ways. But He has a plan, I know that. And I believe something special and good will come from all this, in God's time."

She spoke of God easily, obviously strong in her faith. And he couldn't accuse her of having no adversity in her life. She had a better understanding of the guys and their change of circumstances than most people.

"Can't see it myself," he mumbled. "If God is so loving, why do good men get killed or injured beyond recovery?"

"I can't answer that, but I do hold on to my belief. You're coming to the birthday bash, right?"

Every instinct screamed no. It was one thing to visit a room full of GIs in similar circumstances, another to deliberately put himself in the middle of a crowd of strangers who were normal in every way. He'd have trouble hearing. He'd have trouble coming up with conversation, and he'd feel like a fifth wheel in a room full of people who had known each other all their lives.

"I'll pass," he said.

"George will be disappointed. He was hoping to talk to another soldier, and find out how things are in today's Army. His service was in the forties and fifties. I imagine things have changed a lot since then."

Jack couldn't even imagine warfare back that long ago.

With all the technological advances, he'd bet today's Army was light years from George's.

For a moment he put himself in the other man's shoes. Old, out of touch with friends from the old days. He might be the only one left alive from his service days. A simple request.

He glanced at Allie. She'd comply in a New York minute.

"How about I visit him at his home one afternoon?" Jack offered. One on one, soldier to soldier, he could manage. It was the crowds that were daunting.

"Super. I'll call him tonight and see what he says," Allie said. "And I'll bet he'd love to see Able, as well."

"He did okay today, didn't he?" Jack felt so proud the little fellow had been the perfect visitor. He'd obviously had some obedience training before they found him. And the men had really liked him being there.

"He was perfect. You know there are therapy dogs who go to all kind of places to visit people who normally don't ever see dogs—like old folks homes, convalescent hospitals, the VA. You might consider taking this show on the road."

"One afternoon with guys doesn't mean I need to take him other places. Besides, his stay with me is temporary. Today went okay, but the guys there know me."

"What's that supposed to mean?"

"You try going places where you can't hear half of what's said and see how often you want to jump in," he said.

"Sorry, I hadn't thought about that. You fitted in perfectly at the track open house. And today."

"The guys remember I can't hear well, and they face me

when talking and speak up enough I can hear them. You usually face me when you talk, right?"

"Sorry, I don't think about your hearing loss. I like to look at the people I'm talking to. The open house--"

"I missed a lot today. But since I didn't have to respond, I let it pass and others didn't notice."

"I forget about all that when I'm with you," she said so softly, he almost missed it.

That astonished him. How could anyone forget? He couldn't hear well, he had scars both visible and hidden under his clothes. He couldn't use his right hand and arm for much, walked with a limp and tired easily. He was a mess. And she forgot about it?

Chapter Four

Jack finished shaving and wiped his face with a wet wash cloth. Able sat near him, watching his every move.

"You're lucky, you don't have to shave," Jack told the dog.

Able wagged his tail.

When Jack finished dressing, he went to the kitchen to fix something to eat. His cell phone rang. Surprised, he took it from the counter where he normally left it. Allie was about the only one who had the number.

"Good morning," Allie's voice greeted him when he answered. "I talked to George's granddaughter last evening and he'd love to see you today. I thought I could drive you over since you don't know where he lives."

Jack stared out the window at the back yard.

"Did anyone ever tell you you're pushy?" he asked. He had done more for Allie than anyone else in the last several years. Yet she constantly demanded more. Maybe he should take a stand.

She laughed and he forgot what he was going to say. Her laughter charmed him. Actually, everything about her charmed him. Some stand he'd taken.

"Yeah, I get that a lot. But you wouldn't want to disappoint George, would you?"

"I don't even know him, so why do I care if he's disappointed or not?" He liked teasing her. It was a novel experience for him.

"You'll like him. And he'd really like a visit with someone new. He's told his war stories to everyone in town a dozen times. He'll relish new ears."

"He'll have to talk loud for me to hear him," Jack mumbled.

"He will. I thought around ten would be good. If you don't have other plans."

It was on the tip of his tongue to say he had made other plans. But he couldn't lie. Beside, she'd just push to know what and then he'd be caught out.

"Oh, and bring Able. George will love him, too. See you then," she said, and hung up before he could even make a token protest.

"If we want to live our own lives, we need to plan our attack against Allie the Hun," he explained to Able, as he prepared the dog's meal and set the bowl on the floor. He grabbed a bowl and filled it with cereal, then poured milk over it and stood at the counter, looking out the window and wondering who he was trying to kid as he ate his breakfast.

He'd be a total hermit if left to his own devices. But that didn't mean he had to give into everything Allie planned.

Though the thought of spending more time with her was appealing. She was pretty as could be and seemed to have lots of friends. He couldn't understand why she wanted to push him into mainstream life in Rocky Point. But she did. He could only offer a half-hearted resistance. He'd come to experience life in this small town. The people he'd met were friendly. The open house at the track had been different enough to capture his interest. He'd enjoyed watching the teenagers demonstrate what they'd learned.

The Sheriff and Zack Kincaid had certainly garnered their share of respect and admiration of the community that day. He couldn't remember the names of all the people he'd met. He'd recognized them, though when he saw them again. It was a start.

Jack made sure he and Able were ready when Allie's SUV turned into their driveway. Again not wanting her to get out, he headed for the vehicle and had the back open in no time, the ramp easily pulled out for Able to use.

"He's getting good at that," she commented, when Jack climbed into the passenger seat.

"He'll probably want the ramp even when his leg heals."

"Ummm. Do you want to go to lunch after your visit?" Allie asked, as she backed the car from the drive. "Marcie's place makes the best sandwiches in town."

"I have food at home," Jack said.

"So do I, but her sandwiches are special. I love the shrimp po-boys she makes."

"I can't take Able in a restaurant."

"Oh, I forgot about him." She glanced over her shoulder at Able who was resting his head on the back of the seat. "Sorry, Able."

Jack was glad the dog was along. That settled that.

"I know--Marcie has a patio on the side. It's very popular in the summer months. No one uses it now, but I bet it'll be warm enough today for us to sit out if we're in the sun. And Able can be right on the other side of the low stone wall that encloses the patio."

Jack was torn between a groan and laughter. Allie was a force to be reckoned with.

When they arrived at the home of George's granddaughter, Allie led the way to the front door. In only seconds they were in the house and George was offering his hand to Jack.

The man was in his nineties, yet stood tall and straight. The twinkle in his eyes showed his delight in meeting Jack, and his handshake was firm. He grinned when he met Able. "Always liked dogs. Had a few in my day." He leaned over to pat the dog, then straightened again.

"Come on in. Allie's been telling me all about you. Glad to meet a fellow soldier. Few of us around Rocky Point. Jezzie?" He turned to call.

"I'm getting coffee, Grandpa," a voice came from the back of the house.

"Well, that's right nice of you. We'll be in the sun porch," he called back.

Leading the way through the living room, George gestured to a chair beside the one he took. Jack noticed Allie hadn't come with them. She'd probably gone to help Jezzie, whom he assumed was the granddaughter George lived with.

George sat on his left and smiled again when Jack sat. Was it coincidental or had Allie warned the older man he was deaf in his right ear?

"So, tell me about today's Army. Big changes since I was a GI," George said.

Jack wasn't a story teller. He didn't know what the man wanted to know. After a moment he began with boot camp. Before long the two of them were comparing the similarities and the differences that spanned decades.

Jezzie brought in a tray with hot coffee and some freshly baked cookies. George made introductions and she gave each man a mug of coffee and put the plate of cookies on the small table between them.

"You two help yourselves. Allie and I are visiting in the back. Yell out if you need anything."

* * *

"Wow, Allie, he's cute," Jezzie said, when she returned to the kitchen.

"I know, but I don't think he does."

"Does he make your heart beat a little faster?" Jezzie asked, teasing her friend.

Allie shrugged, uncertain of the special interest she took in Jack. Was she falling for the man? He captured her attention more than anyone she'd ever met since Jason. Her heart ached sometimes for the difficulties he experienced. Other times, she just wanted to have him pull her close and hold her.

"He's nice," she replied lamely.

"You don't usually bring men to see Grandpa, or take them to the community events, so maybe he's more than nice."

"What are you talking about?"

"The track's open house. I've heard from several people that you two were there and cozy, heads together, in a world of your own."

"He's hard of hearing and leans closer to hear. He's new in town. Would you have me ignore him? If I introduce him around, it'll make it easier for him to become part of the community."

"Another hurt critter you're trying to save?" Jezzie poured them each a cup of coffee and went to sit at the island where Allie sat. A plate of cookies was pushed toward Allie. "Eat up, otherwise Grandpa and I will have to eat them all and I don't need the pounds on the hips."

"Like you need to worry."

"What's the real skinny on Jack?"

"I don't know. I want to help him fit in. He lives alone. Doesn't like to get out. He's still self-conscious about the scars and the injuries."

Jezzie nodded. "He's your latest project—save a soldier."

Allie wrinkled her nose. "He's a friend."

"Oh, interesting."

"A romantic involvement is the last thing he's looking for."

"Ah, even more interesting. I just thought you having a new friend was good. Now you're talking romance," Jezzie laughed at Allie's expression. "Hey, chill. It's all good. He's really good looking and maybe just what you need to spark some attraction. Snap him up before the other women in town get a gander."

Allie laughed and reached for a cookie. "In your dreams. Tell me why you're off work today?"

Jezzie worked as a paralegal in the town's primary law office.

"My boss is at a convention in Boston, and I'm caught up at work, so I'm taking some time off. I have a few vacation days on the books and every once in a while I like to splurge and stay home to bake and visit."

"These cookies are great."

"When you leave, I'm making a cake for Grandpa's birthday."

"Which reminds me: I have a list of things I'm bringing; should I also bring ice cream?"

"No, Rhoda is bringing several gallons in an assortment of flavors. If we need more, I'll send someone out on a replenish-the-food run. And Marvel is bringing more cake."

They discussed the birthday party: who was expected, who would miss it. Who was bringing what food.

The time passed swiftly. Once in a while, Allie would glance at the clock, wondering how Jack was doing. Was she being too solicitous? He was a grown man who could take care of himself. If he didn't like visiting with George, he could have found an excuse to leave by now.

It was almost noon when George, Jack and Able came into the kitchen.

"What are you two doing in here?" George asked. "The real action was in the sun room."

"Where you were probably reliving the great battles of World War Two," Jezzie said.

Allie immediately looked at Jack, relieved to see he looked relaxed.

"Shake a leg, girl. We're all going out to lunch. Wear a jacket; we have to sit outside because of the dog."

"Grandpa, I need to make a cake," Jezzie protested.

"Do it later. Jack and Allie are going to Marcie's for lunch and we're invited." The excitement in George's voice reminded Allie the simplest things could be special for some people. She was thrilled Jack had invited George—and that he was going to lunch with her.

Jezzie insisted on driving herself and her grandfather so they wouldn't have to have Allie come back to the house when lunch was over.

The day was sunny and mild. There were a few scattered clouds in the sky, but none overhead to deflect the sun's warmth.

Marcie readily agreed to service on the patio so that Able could be with them.

"Go on around to the gate and I'll let you in. We'll have to wipe down the table and chairs; they haven't been used in weeks. You'll be the only ones there—take the dog in. He won't bother anyone else."

"No health issues?" Jack asked.

Marcie shook her head. "Service dogs are allowed in all the time. Allie says Able's a well-behaved dog; it'll be fine."

George again sat at Jack's left. Allie sat on his right and Jezzie sat opposite him.

Jack ordered the shrimp po-boy like Allie, while George ordered a ham and cheese and Jezzie a Cobb salad.

Able lay down beside Jack and rested his head on the toe of Jack's shoe. In only seconds he was asleep.

"Good mannered dog," George said.

Jack explained how he came to have him, nodding toward Allie. "She's going to take him once his leg heals and see if she can find a home for him."

"Seems like he has a good home right where he is," George said.

Jack glanced at Allie. She smiled at him. He went instantly on alert. That wasn't her normal smile—more like a cat-who-got-the-canary smile.

"When he's well, he goes to you," Jack said firmly.

She nodded. "Of course, that was the agreement and I always stick to my agreements."

"It's supposed to rain tomorrow," Jezzie said oblivious to the interchange. "And the temperature's going to drop. This might be the last day we can enjoy eating outside until spring."

"Hate it when it rains," George said. "Makes all my joints ache."

"We need the rain, however," Allie said. "It's been a dry fall. We don't want everything dying off for lack of water."

"There'll be plenty of storms coming in winter. Another week or so of Indian summer would have been nice," Jezzie said. "Jack, are you from around here? Maine, I mean."

"No, the Midwest originally, but the last twelve years I've been in the Army. I've been stationed at different bases all around the country."

"Most recently Afghanistan," Allie said.

He nodded.

The thick sandwiches were eaten with relish as conversation ebbed and flowed. Shortly after everyone finished, Allie leaned back in her chair. "This has been fun. We'll have to do it again."

"Thanks for including us," Jezzie said with a smile. "I know Grandpa liked having company and then this treat." She looked at Jack, "You two seemed to be talking up a storm earlier."

"Had things to compare, girl. Jack's all right," George said.

"High praise," Jezzie murmured, with a smile at Jack.

"Are you coming tomorrow, son?" George asked.

"Wasn't planning on it," Jack said. "I'll wish you a happy birthday today."

"Ah, come on, don't leave me to the rest of the town. Except for that Wentworth boy, there's no one else to talk with."

"Grandpa, you have lots of friends in town," Jezzie said.

"Yeah, but most of the other service men served in the Navy or Marines." He said it with a frown, which had the rest smiling at the pride he had in the Army.

Allie looked at Jack expectantly. "Maybe I can persuade him to change his mind," she said.

He slowly shook his head, but didn't say anything.

* * *

"George must have really enjoyed your visit. I don't remember when I saw him so animated. It has to be hard to grow old when so many of your friends and families have gone on before you. He's lucky Jezzie's so devoted to him," Allie said, as they watched George and Jezzie drive away.

Allie remembered when Jack had told her he had no one. She tried to imagine being all alone in the world. She'd never be totally alone as long as she had the Lord with her. But to be without her parents, grandparents, aunts and uncles and cousins? Hard to imagine, since they all had been a part of her life since she was born.

"He had all girls, you know. And they had all girls. I think he would have loved a son or grandson to follow in his footsteps."

"What did he do after he got out of the Army?" Jack asked.

"You didn't talk about that?"

"No, just reminisced about the service, and how different it is today with all the technology compared to his days serving."

"He was in insurance. Had a nice business, which his oldest daughters took over when he wanted to retire. There's a big age gap between his oldest daughter and Jezzie's mom. Charlotte is old enough to retire herself soon. But Jezzie's mom is only in her fifties. She works for her sister and I expect she'll take over when Charlotte does retire."

"Continuity." Jack had led a nomadic life. He had no strong ties to the place he grew up, no family, no friends there anymore. He'd lost touch with the ones from high school. How different would his life have been had his parents lived at least until he finished school? He'd never know. He wasn't one to dwell on might-have-beens.

When Allie pulled into the driveway at Jack's house, they got Able out of the back of the SUV using the makeshift ramp.

"Thanks for going today," she said, leaning against the car. "I wish you'd think about tomorrow. It'll be a fun gathering and a good chance to meet more people."

Able ran toward the house with his hobbling, lurching gait. Jack watched him and then looked at Allie.

"Today was one thing. If I couldn't hear George, I'd just say so. Tomorrow with all the people and commotion, I'd miss out on most of the conversations. People don't want to keep repeating themselves."

He didn't want to admit the real reason—he'd feel like a fish out of water around neighbors who had known each other all their lives. Granted the reason he'd moved here was to see what the town was like. But blending in was impossible.

"If you change your mind it's at the church fellowship hall. Starts at one o'clock." She gave him a smile and called farewell to Able. Turning she got back in her car and once Jack moved out of her way, backed out.

He watched her drive away, wondering why he'd wished she'd tried to persuade him to go. He'd made up his mind and his decision was firm.

The longing to be in her good graces surprised him. She hadn't said anything to show she was disappointed. But he felt as if he'd let her down.

Relationships with women were always complicated. He'd been in a couple where he thought they had a future, but something always came up to make him step back. Being transferred every couple of years also put a damper on any long-term relationships. Not that he'd found anyone to make a lasting commitment with. Not that he understood women. Give him his buddies any day.

* * *

The birthday celebration for George was in full swing the next afternoon, when Rachel nudged Allie. "Look who just came in. I thought you said he wasn't coming," she said in a low voice.

The two of them stood behind the punch table serving cups of the iced cold beverage. Kids ran around laughing and chasing each other. Small groups stood talking here and there in the large room. George sat in a chair at one end of the room surrounded by friends. From the laughter coming from there, he and the others were enjoying themselves. Despite the change in the weather, most of the people had braved the rain and come to celebrate with their oldest veteran.

Allie looked over and saw Jack hesitating by the door. Even as she watched it seemed as if he'd had second thoughts and was about to leave before anyone else saw him.

"I'll be back," she said, and hastily hurried over to the door.

"Hi, I'm glad you came," she said reaching out to touch

him, to verify he'd really shown up. "George will be delight-ed."

He looked at her, then glanced around the room. "Is the entire town here?"

She laughed. "Pretty much. Or at least a good percent-age. And it's a drop in affair, so people will be coming and going all afternoon. Come and get some punch and maybe some of the birthday cake, then I'll get you through the crowd around George so he'll know you made it."

"I'll pass on the refreshments. Maybe this was a bad idea."

"Not at all. Come on." Allie linked her free arm through his and began walking across the large hall. Occasionally someone called out a greeting to Jack. He nodded in return, recognizing some faces from the day at the track.

"George, look who came after all," Allie said, as she ap-proached the guest of honor.

"Hey, boy, glad to see you. Jezzie, get a chair for Jack. Connor, this is the other Army man in town. Jack, meet Connor Wentworth. He served in this man's army, too."

Jezzie push a chair closer so Jack could sit with Connor and her grandfather, then scooted around the group and headed back to the refreshment table with Allie.

"I'm surprised to see Jack," Jezzie said.

"Me, too. He said he wouldn't come. I wonder why he changed his mind."

"I bet Conner's glad he did. He's heard Grandpa's stories a hundred times."

When there was a lull in the demand for punch and cake,

Allie took her digital camera and wandered around taking candid shots. Some she'd give to George, a few might hit the local paper as a write up of the celebration. She snapped a couple of Jack and George together. She might keep one or two of those for herself. She tried to capture the expressions as they talked. Once George said something and everyone laughed—including Jack. It almost took away her breath. He was so good looking. He should laugh more often.

Allie was studying the photos, making sure she captured as many faces as possible so no one felt neglected, when Harriet Lodge touched her on the shoulder. She turned and smiled at Jason's mother.

"Hi, did you just get here?" she asked, giving her a quick hug.

"No, actually Paul and I have been here a few minutes. I haven't seen you in a week or two. Come with me to the refreshment table. I'd like some of the birthday cake. Sorry we weren't here when it was cut."

"I was afraid the candles would set the church on fire. Jezzie insisted on one for each year. I think the fire department was standing by."

"And did George blow them all out?" Harriet asked.

"With a little help from the kids gathered around. I loved the contrast—little Tommy Cartwright, who is what now, about five? And George. I got a great shot of that."

Once Harriet had her cake and punch, she and Allie moved to one of the vacant tables at the side of the hall.

"Who's that man with George?" she asked once they were seated.

"You mean Jack?"

Harriet looked at her in surprise. "You know him?"

"He recently moved here. He staying in the Stafford place out at the end of Water Street."

"So he's a stranger in town." Harriet glanced back at him.

Allie looked at Harriet. "He's a newcomer. He's been here a few weeks. I invited him today so he can meet more people. He was at the track open house."

"I'd be careful, or people will get the wrong impression," the older woman said, looking over at the group around George.

Allie studied her for a moment. "What kind of wrong impression?" she asked.

"That there's more going on than there is. We don't know this man. If he's renting the Stafford place, it's likely he'll move on once the weather turns bad. That house gets the worst of the storms from the sea."

"I don't want him to move along," Allie said involuntarily, looking at Jack.

Harriet frowned. "Nonsense, he's a stranger. What does it matter if he moves on or not?"

"I like him." She met the older woman's eyes.

Harriet's expression went hard. "He's hardly Jason."

Allie took a deep breath. She'd faced this before. Every time she'd gone on a date, Harriet had something to say. To Jason's mother, his memory was sacrosanct. It was as if he had gone to the store and would return any minute.

"I know," she said gently. "But Jason's gone. We still miss

him, but he's forever gone."

Harriet reached out to pat Allie's hand. "But the love you two shared will always be."

"I loved Jason. But love is like a candle--lighting another candle doesn't diminish the flame of the first. I'd like to think I have a lot of love to give."

Harriet wasn't mollified. Allie suspected Jason's mother expected her to be true to his memory forever. She'd always miss her first love, but she had moved on. She wanted whatever life had to offer. If his mother had her way, she'd remain celibate the rest of her life in memory of a young man who had not had a chance to live beyond his teen years.

Allie knew she wasn't a top candidate for a man to fall in love with, but she still hoped secretly that someday some man would see through her limitations to the real her and want to join his life with hers forever. If that wasn't to be, she didn't want to remain single out of a misguided loyalty to a teenage love.

"Hi Sweetie. Sorry we're late. We had a flat tire, can you imagine? Your father wanted to fix it but I insisted we call for help. He'd have gotten his clothes all dirty and then we'd have had to go home while he changed and been even later." Allie's mother gave her a hug and smiled at the other woman.

"How are you, Harriet?"

"Doing fine, Penny. You?"

"Doing fine as well." She turned to survey the party. "Looks like a good turnout."

"People have been coming and going since one o'clock," Allie said. "I should get back to help Rachel with the punch."

As she turned, her dad came up and gave her a hug. "Where're you off to?" he asked.

"Going to help at the punch table. Want some?"

"I do. Hello, Harriet. Can I get you ladies some punch?" he asked the two older women.

When both said yes, he walked with Allie to the punch bowls. Once he had his cups balanced and turned away, Allie glanced over at the table where her mother sat. The two women had their heads together and were looking straight at Jack.

"Great," she said under her breath.

"What?" Rachel asked. She scooped up a ladle of punch and poured into a waiting cup.

When they were alone, Allie turned to her friend. "Harriet thinks my being friends with Jack will give the wrong impression."

"Does it give any impression?"

"She thinks it means I'm being disloyal to Jason's memory."

"Give me a break. I know you two were tight in high school, but that was years ago. Who knows now if you'd even would have stayed together once you went off to college? Does she expect you to devote your life to his memory instead of having a life of your own?'

"Probably. She usually has some comment if she learns I've dated anyone."

"I think your Jack's handsome as can be, in a rugged manly way. If he lights up your world, why not see where it'll lead?"

"Lights up my world? Where do you get these ideas?" Allie glanced at him. He was handsome, despite the scars which she couldn't even see from this distance.

"I say it from watching you around him. Your eyes light up, your face seems happier. I don't know, there's a glow around the two of you. He acts as if he can't keep his eyes off you."

"Don't ever say that around Harriet. Or my mother come to that. Beside, he's probably just focusing on what I'm saying because of his hearing loss."

Rachel smiled slyly. "It's not from hearing loss."

"He's a new resident I'm just trying to make feel at home."

"I don't remember you taking this much interest in Faith when she was a newcomer," Rachel said, referring to the Sheriff's fiancee who had only been in town a few months.

"She wasn't isolating herself," Allie said petulantly. "Anyway, I'm just trying to make him feel at home."

"So he'll stay."

Allie shrugged. She was interested in Jack more than anyone knew. But it was because she recognized a fellow sufferer. He had been through worse than she'd ever experienced and needed a hand to fit in to the peaceful world of Rocky Point. Anyone would want to help.

But she couldn't help sneaking another glance in his direction.

He sat next to George, nodding at something the man said. From here he looked as strong and healthy as anyone else in the room. And he was handsome. In fact, he was the best looking man she'd ever seen. His dark blue eyes looked so solemn. He rarely smiled. But when he did, it transformed him and caused an odd flutter deep within her.

She wanted to see him smile more.

At her.

She blinked at the idea and looked away, catching Harriet's eye as the woman stared at her. Over the years her family had included Jason's family in many holidays. They were as close as if she and Jason had married.

But they hadn't. The accident had robbed the town of several bright and promising young men and woman. Being the only survivor had been a burden not of her choosing. It was hard to epitomize the lives of those who had died. Her parents had wanted to cosset her. The parents of those teens who had died in the crash looked to her life as a representation of what their own children might have become.

She tried to live her life the best she could with the Lord's help. But she didn't want to short change herself for those of her friends who had died ten years ago. And she didn't believe the Lord wanted that either.

"Time to take a stand," she murmured, feeling the stirring of rebellion building.

"You go, girl," Rachel said with a broad smile. "Live life abundantly. That's what the Lord wants us to do. He didn't spare you from the crash to live life any way but to the fullest."

"I feel like I'm living for Jason and Britta and Mary Ellen, and all the others who died that day. I watch what I do, am always there for their parents."

"In a way you are—but only if you live the abundant life the Lord has for you. Stifling any aspect to please someone else is not what you should be doing. They were here for a short time, true. But you can't be all things to their parents. You need to be here for you alone."

"Is that what I've been doing—trying to be something to the parents?"

"Maybe not consciously, but I see you at every event, talking with the parents of those who died. I don't see you talking with many eligible men. If you like Jack and he likes you, why not see where it'll lead?"

"I'm not sure he likes me very much. And I'm a long way from deciding anything like that with him or anyone else," Allie said.

If the truth were told, however, if only to herself-she was fascinated by Jack Donner and wanted to get to know him better. The thought of him leaving Rocky Point filled her with a mild panic. She didn't know him that well, but what she did know she liked. He'd served his country when needed. He was loyal to the men at the VA Hospital. She knew he hadn't wanted to come today, but he had—for George. That was a tremendous act of kindness. She respected a man who put others ahead of his own feelings.

"Take him some punch. He's probably thirsty by now. And maybe sit and flirt a little," Rachel suggested. "I can take care of things here. It's just refills for the most part now."

"Okay." Allie liked the idea. She could sit with him and listen as he and George swapped stories. Carefully carrying two cups of punch on a tray, she made her way across the fellowship hall.

"Excuse me, I've brought punch for the birthday boy and his friend," she said, sliding in through the crowd. George reached for his and took a long drink. Jack nodded his thanks and took a cup, sipping cautiously.

"It's good," he said, drinking the rest.

Someone moved and offered her a chair. She sat and leaned her cane against the back. "So what have I missed?" she asked.

"George and Jack are trying to outdo each other with stories of boot camp. If they aren't exaggerating, then I wouldn't want to be at any boot camp if it was as arduous as these guys make it sound," one of the men from the church said with a grin. "Tell the truth, guys, it wasn't all hard work, was it?"

The two former Army men looked at each other. Jack winked. "We're softening it some so as not to scare you," he said solemnly.

George laughed and nodded. "It was worse."

"You did have downtime," someone called. "What did you do then?"

"Liberty. Ahh, can't be telling all that with the ladies around," George said with a twinkle in his eye. "Just remember we were young back then. Not so smart as we are now."

Jack smiled slightly, glancing at Allie.

She felt her heart kick over. Smiling back she wondered if he had spent his liberty in wild ways, or was just feeding into the crowd's fantasy. Maybe she'd ask him when they were alone.

"There you are, Allie. Paul and I were talking about a memorial garden for Jason. We want your input. I'm sure these folks would excuse you." Harriet stood beside her chair, her gaze compelling as she stared down at Allie.

Instantly feeling on the defensive, Allie nodded. "Of course. I'll be right there."

Harriet didn't move, so Allie reached for her cane. "Save some of the stories for me," she said as she rose and turned to accompany Harriet.

Once they were away from the group, Allie said, "I didn't know you were planning a memorial garden. When did this idea come up?"

"Recently. Of course we want your input since you and Jason were so close. I know you miss him as much as we do, if not more. It's hard to lose someone so young."

"He was special," Allie concurred, wondering if the memorial garden could be discussed at another time. This was supposed to be a celebration for George's birthday. Yet, just as Rachel had said, she was following along, feeling guilty she had not died in that crash, trying to appease Harriet. Wishing she could fill the shoes of the teenagers who had perished.

"I can't help thinking about the grandchildren we might have now had Jason lived," Harriet said. "We'll never have any to gladden our old age."

"You're not that old. Besides, there are programs for people who want to be grandparents to foster children or to be grandparents to children who are in orphanages."

"They wouldn't be Jason's children."

"But they would love to have grandparents and give as much love as natural born children would."

Harriet didn't respond to that.

"Where's Paul?" Allie asked, glancing around. She spotted him with a group of men she knew loved fishing. They looked deep in discussion.

"He's busy. We'll get him later." She led the way back to Allie's mother and the two vacant chairs she was saving.

"Are you in on the garden plan, too?" Allie asked her mom as she sat beside her.

"What garden?"

"The memorial garden I thought we should plant in memory of Jason," Harriet said taking the other vacant chair. "Something suitable that would honor his short life."

"And the others from the crash?" Allie asked.

Her mom nodded. "That's a great idea. Why didn't we think of something like this before? Where would you put it?"

"I thought on our property, near the sidewalk."

"Not central enough," Allie's mom said. "I suggest we ask Pastor John if we could use a portion of the grounds near the Sunday school rooms. Everyone would see it at least once a week, and if we put some benches in it people could come for quiet contemplation or prayer."

"I thought a more personal tribute," Harriet began.

"I like the idea of one for all who died. It was a church outing. Everyone in that van was from our church. This way we can remember everybody," Penny said enthusiastically.

Allie looked at Harriet. The older woman frowned. She

smiled gently and reached out to touch her. "I think that's a great idea. But really, you don't need me involved. That's something all the parents of those who died should have some say in," she said softly.

"I'd think you'd want some say in what we do. Jason and you were in love, planning to marry," she said stiffly.

Allie nodded. "But I was only eighteen. Who knows what might have happened once we'd gone to separate colleges, once we'd met new friends, once our lives had gone in different directions."

Harriet looked shocked. "I know Jason would have always loved you."

"And I might have always loved him, or we might have changed. No one knows the future but God. I think the memorial garden is a good idea, but not one I need to be involved in," Allie said, standing. "I hope such a garden will give you solace in Jason's death. He would not have wanted you to grieve so long."

"So you walk away. Where, back to that stranger?"

"He's a new resident. A stranger is only a friend not yet met." Allie felt a wave of guilt sweep over her. There was nothing wrong in befriending Jack. Nothing she did could change the past, but the future beckoned and maybe it was time she looked forward.

"He won't stay. He wasn't born and raised here. He has no ties. Once he's better, he'll leave. You mark my words," Harriet said bitterly.

Allie walked away, but not toward Jack where she longed to go. She returned to the punch bowl. "Take a break,

Rachel, my turn to man this station."

"What did Harriet say? I saw her lecturing you. And I have to admire the way she cut you out of the group with Jack. Jealous maybe?"

"Maybe. I didn't realize before today how much she still thinks of me and Jason as a couple."

"Told you so."

"No one likes someone who says that," Allie said with a grin to her friend. "Go on and mix and mingle. I'll stay away from all dicey areas and serve punch to one and all."

"Don't let her intimidate you. You have every right to your own life. Maybe even more than some of us."

"Yes, Mom."

Rachel laughed as she left the table and went to talk with friends.

Allie was content to stay behind the table, as if it were a buffer from the emotions she felt on the other side. She watched Jack for a few minutes. Several more people had joined the group surrounding them, including Michelle Carson and Laura Halton. Michelle was a nurse visiting her aunt. Laura had lived in Rocky Point her entire life. She was a couple of years younger than Allie, but they knew each other well enough. Allie wondered what they were talking about. Both focused on Jack as if he was the best thing they'd seen in ages. Which he probably was. He laughed at something one of them said and glanced at George, who was grinning from ear to ear.

Deliberately forcing her gaze elsewhere, she looked over to her mother. Harriet still sat with her and looked as if she were bending her ear about something. Probably her.

She had a fondness for Jason's mother, but had she let Harriet have more influence on her life than was warranted?

"Another cup for the road?" Jack asked. Allie turned and found him standing there with his cup in his left hand. Michelle stood beside him smiling.

"I'll have some, too. Jack said it's good," she said.

"Refreshing," Allie murmured filling Jack's cup and handed a freshly filled one to Michelle. "How long are you visiting?"

"For a while, I think—now that I've met Jack. I'm between jobs. Auntie asked me to visit while I wait to hear about some applications I've sent out."

Jack watched Michelle as she talked. Allie couldn't tell if he was being polite, or because he was having trouble hearing her, or because she fascinated him.

When he finished the punch, he looked around as for a place to set it down.

"I can take it if you're finished," she said holding out her hand.

He handed the empty cup to her. "I'm heading out."

"I'm glad you came. Did you enjoy yourself?" she asked. He nodded.

"Laura's not ready to go, but I am. Can I get a lift from you?" Michelle asked, putting her cup down and looking directly at Jack.

"Sure."

Allie swallowed hard. She should be happy Jack had come and met more people. That was what she'd hoped for, that he'd begin to become assimilated into the community. But Michelle was only a visitor. How would that help?

He glanced around the room, pausing when his gaze met the glaring eyes of Harriet Lodge. "Not sure everyone was glad I came," he said, looking back at Allie.

"Maybe, but not because of who you are, but of what you represent. Others are glad to welcome you. One Sunday you might like to come to church."

"I always go to church when visiting Auntie. Maybe we could both go tomorrow," Michelle said brightly.

"I'll see." He looked at Allie for a long moment as if memorizing every inch of her face. Then turned. "See you."

Allie watched as they walked away, wishing she could go with him. Wishing she could have asked for a ride home. Just to learn more about how he liked the party. To find out what he thought of Rocky Point and if he was considering leaving.

Harriet's gaze also followed the couple as they left together. Her face seemed to relax.

Allie took stock. Did everyone in town think she still longed for Jason? That she wouldn't find another man to love, to have a family with?

Time to set that straight. And maybe find she and Jack had more in common than a limp!

Chapter Five

Allie sat down to her computer the next afternoon to review all the pictures she'd taken at the birthday celebration. Slowly going through each one, she noted the shots she especially liked. Ones that would never see the light of day she deleted instantly. Then she began to review again with a view to crop for the best effect. She paused on one of Jack where he was looking directly into the camera. His expression was solemn, his eyes dark and mysterious. She noted that as one she especially wanted to enlarge. There was one with Jack and George that she studied. Liking the contrast of the old soldier and the young, she planned to send that one to the paper. And make an enlarged copy for George.

Would Jack want one? Probably. She'd print up a bunch and maybe take them by his place later.

He hadn't been in church that morning. She didn't know if she was happy he hadn't joined Michelle, or sad because he'd missed a really good sermon from Pastor John on the commandment about loving parents to live long upon the earth.

She'd been sitting with her parents, and gave thanks for them and the way they always were there for her. She knew they still saw her as their little girl, and added a short prayer to ask for wisdom to let them know she was an adult and fully responsible for herself.

Allie played music as she cropped, sized and printed picture after picture. While making a living at photography, she was always sharing candid shots with people. She loved their delight when they unexpectedly received some photographs. She didn't believe it cut into her business at all and hoped it spread good will.

It was dinner time when she finished. She went to the kitchen, but saw nothing that appealed. Excited about seeing the pictures earlier, she'd skipped eating with her parents after church. Now she decided to see if her mom would let her come for supper. She gave her a quick call.

"Spaghetti, your favorite," her mom said when Allie asked.

"Enough for me to join you?"

"Of course. I always prepare enough for leftovers as your dad loves them so. There's plenty. We're eating in about thirty minutes."

"I'll be there."

* * *

Allie let herself in her old home and followed the delicious aroma back to the kitchen. Her mother stirred the sauce as it bubbled on the stove.

"Hi, Honey. Glad you decided to join us. Did you get all your pictures printed?"

"I did, but it took all afternoon." She laid an envelope on the counter. "I brought you and Dad some. I didn't get as many of you as I thought I had."

"Heavens, we do not need our pictures taken. I hope you got some good ones of George and Jezzie."

"I did. I included one cute one in every packet so we'll all remember why we were there. Need any help?"

"If you want to set the table and call your father, we'll be ready to eat in no time."

Once grace had been said, her father asked about her afternoon. Allie brought him up to speed. Then he asked, "What do you know about Jack Donner?"

Allie glanced at her mother who was concentrating on serving the plates. "He's a veteran. Injured in Afghanistan. Just released from the VA Hospital in Portland."

"Donner. He from around here? I don't recognize the name."

"No, he's originally from the Midwest. But he has no parents and decided to get a place near to Portland."

"We're not so near," her mother said.

"Nearer than the Midwest," her father responded. He looked at her. "You meet him up at the hospital?"

"No, I met him at the grocery store, actually."

"Heard of that happening."

"Paul, it's not the same thing," her mother said.

"What? I just said I've heard of people meeting at the grocery store."

"As if it means something more."

He frowned. "More than what?"

"Nothing. Pass the garlic bread please. Allie, Harriet talked with Pastor John after church this morning and he's all for the memorial garden. We'd like you to be on the committee planning it. Once we have a concrete plan, we'll present it to the church and see how we can get funding."

"Who else is on the committee?"

"Does it matter?" her mother asked in surprise.

"Yes. I think it should be for those who lost a child. Not me."

"I thought you'd be glad to be a part of it. For Jason."

"Now you sound like Harriet," Allie said.

Penny looked at her husband in question. He shook his head. "Don't get me involved in this. What she says makes sense. I don't think anyone from this family should be on it; our daughter lived."

"Yes, but she was part of that youth group. I think we should be involved."

"You do it, Mom. I don't want to."

"Allie, I know Harriet and the others would like you there."

"Not this time."

"Let her be, Penny. She said no. That's the end of it," her father said.

"Is it that new man in town?" her mom asked.

Allie shook her head.

Her mother didn't look convinced.

"Didn't George look happy to have so many come celebrate his birthday? I hope I'm still here when I'm as old has he is, and as spry," her father said, deliberately changing the subject.

Allie smiled. "I'm sure you'll still be kicking like George. He did have a grand time. Jezzie said today he said it was the best party he's ever been to."

Gradually, the tension eased and the rest of the meal passed harmoniously.

Allie helped with the dishes, hoping her mother would not bring up either Jack or the proposed memorial. She kept the conversation firmly on other topics and once the dishes were finished, she said goodbye.

The more she thought about what Rachel had said, the more she could see many people in town had an image of her as pining for Jason. She was the miracle who had survived the crash. Would she forever be set apart because of it? She did not want to be singled out. It had been a miracle, one that she often thanked the Lord for. But she wanted to be free of close scrutiny, free to live her life as she saw fit, not always as a representative of those friends who were now gone.

* * *

The next morning Allie called Pastor John. "Can I come by today to talk to you?" she asked.

"Sure. About the memory garden?"

Even the pastor thought she should be involved.

"No. Well, partly."

"Ten o'clock suit you?"

"Yes. Thank you."

Promptly at ten, Allie knocked on the opened door to

his office and stepped inside.

"Good morning," she said with a smile.

"Good morning, come on in. Want to shut the door?"

"Yes." She closed it gently behind her and went to sit down across the desk from her pastor.

"Serious stuff, huh?" he asked.

"I think so. And it came to me all at once, at George's birthday party. Something Rachel said." She hesitated, trying to get the words right.

"And that was?" he prompted.

"That I was living my life for all those who died in the crash ten years ago. That I didn't live life to the fullest as Christ wants, but am trying to please all the parents of all the kids on that minivan. If that's what I'm doing, I want to stop."

He nodded, leaning back in his chair, his expression thoughtful.

"And do you think that's what you're doing?" he asked.

She shrugged. "I don't know. I thought I was living like I wanted. But Rachel says I'm always going out of my way to talk to the parents, to follow their suggestions."

"Maybe you're being kind to them. They lost so much."

"Harriet thinks I should be thinking of Jason all the time. I don't think she's moved on."

Pastor John nodded. "I expect this has something to do with the latest town resident."

"Jack." She nodded. "You're right. She really dislikes my being friendly with him. It's not like I haven't dated other men since Jason died. He's new, and I've only been trying to include him in things so he'll fit in. Somehow she sees that as wrong."

"Maybe Harriet should try some kindness to new residents," he said dryly.

She grinned. "I don't think she likes him very much."

"Because he's the first man who seriously competes with Jason, in her eyes."

"That's what Rachel said." Was it true? She hadn't felt like this with the others she'd dated over the years. Every day Jack became more special to her. Did it show?

"How do you feel?" the pastor asked.

"About Jack?"

"About him and Harriet, and the parents of your former school mates?"

"I have great affection for Harriet and the other parents. They were so supportive and helpful when I was recovering. I missed all the funerals, you know. I wish I could have been there to say goodbye, but I wasn't able to be."

"I believe they look at you and see what their own children could have become. But my guess is most of them would be quite distressed to learn you felt you had to do anything to please them," he said.

"Harriet thinks my love for Jason should still be strong."

"What do you think?"

"I don't even know if we would be together today. We had lots in common in high school. But he was going to college a year ahead of me. I was planning on a different college. We might have gotten married eventually, or maybe not. But Harriet seems to think we were an endless love and can't understand how I could ever be interested in someone else."

"My advice to you is pray for guidance from the Lord. Listen to what He tells you and go forth and do it. Shall we pray together now?"

Allie nodded, bowing her head, feeling as if a huge weight was lifted from her shoulders. The pastor prayed for wisdom, as she had last night. And for the path the Lord wanted her on to be made clear.

"Thank you, Pastor John. I feel much better," she said as she was getting ready to leave.

"Invite that young man to church."

"I have. I will again," she said with a smile.

Leaving the church, Allie knew exactly what she was going to do that afternoon--visit Jack. Share the photos she'd made for him, and invite him to church again.

* * *

Allie had the all the ingredients she needed for baking, so she made a batch of cupcakes to take when she visited Jack. She frosted each one and carefully put them on a tray. With the envelope of photos, she was ready to go.

She looked forward to seeing him again and hearing how he and Able were getting along. She still hoped he'd bond with the dog and keep him once the cast came off his leg. If not, she'd take Able, but she thought he would suit Jack more.

When she arrived at the house at the end of the road, she was surprised to see a small sports car in the driveway.

He already had a visitor. She debated turning around and going home, but knew they had been alerted to her arrival by Able's barking. Even though it was twenty degrees colder today than last week, two people were sitting on the porch and Able stood at the top of the ramp barking. She parked to one side, and picked up the tray and envelope.

She recognized Michelle once she left the car. Ignoring the slight twinge of jealousy, Allie took her cane and, balancing the tray with the envelope under her arm, she started for the porch.

Jack came down the stairs to meet her, reaching with his good hand for the tray. He wore a thick sweater over his shirt and looked as if he was enjoying the invigorating weather. At least the rain had moved on and the sun shone from a blue sky.

"Hi," she said feeling almost breathless at his smile.

"Hi back," he said. "These look good."

"A little something." Their gazes held for a moment.

Michelle stood at the top of the stairs. "Great minds think alike, I brought him a cake." She wore a short jacket and tailored slacks. Her hair was tossed a little from the breeze.

"Then I hope you don't overdose on sugar," Allie said, feeling a bit disappointed her treat wasn't the only one he'd received today.

"Hi, Michelle," Allie said when she reached the steps.

"Come up and sit down. It's a little cool, but we're sheltered from the breeze here. I'll put those in the kitchen for you if you like, Jack," she said, reaching for the tray. "Save you the trip." She smiled brightly and went inside like she was the hostess or something.

"I brought you some pictures from the birthday party," Allie said, as she sat on the edge of one of the Adirondack chairs. She dare not slide all the way back if she wanted to make any kind of graceful exit. She held out the envelope just as Michelle returned.

"Thanks," Jack said. He sat on another chair and opened the envelope with one hand, letting the photos slide out onto his lap.

"Oh, these are fantastic!" Michelle said, leaning over him, resting her hand on his shoulder as she gazed at the pictures.

Allie wasn't sure, but she thought he stiffened a bit with the familiar touch.

"I didn't know you were going to be here, Michelle, or I'd have looked for some with you in them. I can bring them to church next Sunday."

"That would be fantastic. I'm sure you must have taken a couple of me sitting with Jack and George. Those would be the ones I want." She gave Allie a friendly smile.

Allie nodded, trying to remember if she had taken any such shots.

Michelle moved to sit next to Jack, drawing her chair just a bit closer. "I came to offer my assistance if he needed any help. I am a nurse, you know. I almost got the job at the town's clinic. Then I would have met Jack even earlier, when he first moved here."

"Aren't you visiting your aunt?" Allie asked, wondering

what the story was about the clinic job. As far as she knew, Faith had been their top pick, even though Michelle's aunt worked as the receptionist at the clinic.

"I'm here for an indefinite stay. I'm looking for a new job and thought I might as well visit my aunt while I have the time. I'm so glad I did. I wouldn't have met Jack otherwise."

She beamed at him and he nodded slowly, still looking at the pictures.

"It was a nice party," Allie said, after a moment of awkward silence. Maybe she should leave.

Able came over and dropped a ball at her feet, then look at her with pleading eyes.

"Should you be playing catch with your leg in a cast?" she asked the dog, eying the tennis ball.

"I checked with the vet. He said the dog probably won't do anything to injure the leg, and it's hard to keep Border collies inactive."

"He's such a beautiful dog. I wish I could have a dog, but I live in an apartment in Portland and once I'm working again, I wouldn't have time for one. Here, Able, come here and I'll throw the ball for you," Michelle said.

Able stared at the tennis ball, then looked up at Allie. She smiled and reached for the damp ball, rolling it down the ramp and into the yard. The dog scampered after it, his injured leg held off the ground.

"He seems to manage fine on three legs," she murmured.

Another awkward silence, then Allie smiled at Michelle and tried another topic. "So, where are you looking for work?"

"Portland mainly. It's not so far from here," Michelle responded, looking at Jack. When he didn't meet her gaze, she looked back at Allie. "If not there, then any of the small towns between here and there. I want to stay close to my aunt, you know," she said, her gaze flicking toward Jack again.

"Have you tried the VA Hospital?" Allie asked.

Michelle slowly shook her head. "There's an idea. I was hoping to be an obstetrics nurse, help deliver babies. That's the best part of nursing."

Jack replaced the pictures in the envelope and placed it on the small table by his chair. "You're obviously great at your job, those are excellent pictures."

"Thank you." Time to go. Allie couldn't think of another thing to say. She wanted to ask Jack how he was doing. Would he like to come to church next Sunday? Did he want to go to the VA hospital with her again this week? But not in front of Michelle.

She rose. "I'll be going. I just came to give you the pictures."

"That was really sweet of you," Michelle said with a smile.

"I'll walk you to your car," Jack said, standing abruptly. "I'll be right back," he said to Michelle.

They walked to the car in silence.

"Thanks for coming by. I didn't know Michelle was coming." He shook his head. "And I don't know how to get her to leave."

Allie burst out laughing. "Really? Just tell her you need a

nap."

"She'll offer to tuck me in."

She giggled again. "A big tough soldier like you can handle Michelle. She's nice enough, if a bit pushy."

He gazed into her eyes. "Pushy? I guess that's one word for it."

"Want to come to church on Sunday?" she asked, remembering her plan to invite him. "I'll introduce you around and maybe we could go to dinner at the café afterward. Have a day away from your own cooking." She almost held her breath, wanting him to agree so much.

"What for?"

She blinked. Why did most people go to church—to worship the Lord.

"For worship and fellowship."

He shook his head. "I'm not much on God right now."

She reached out to touch his arm. "I'd think you'd be so grateful to be alive that you'd want to give thanks every day."

"What about the men who didn't make it back? What about the wives and children who won't ever see them again? Doesn't sound like something to be grateful for," he said bitterly.

"I know what you're feeling. That's how I felt after the crash. Of the nine of us, I was the only one who lived. I don't know why. But I do know I'm very grateful for the life I have, for family and friends and the strength that comes from the Lord."

Michelle walked down the steps. "What are you two talking about? If you're not leaving, Allie, you should come back up and sit down."

Allie smiled, wishing she hadn't interrupted, but what was done was done. "I'm leaving. I was inviting Jack to church Sunday."

"I've already done so," Michelle said joining them. "He said no, but I'm not giving up." She smiled up at him. "Maybe one day."

He shook his head again.

"You never know what the future holds," Allie said. She bid them both goodbye and got in her car. Rolling down the window, she said, "I'm going to the VA on Thursday, want to go with me? You and Able? He was such a hit last time."

Jack hesitated a moment, then nodded. "Sure, I don't have a lot of pressing engagements just now."

She laughed softly, wanting to reach out and hug him. But conscious of Michelle standing there, she smiled and nodded. "Okay, I'll swing by and pick you up same time."

As she drove back to town, Allie couldn't help wishing Thursday was coming earlier rather than later in the week. One glance as she pulled out of the driveway showed Michelle arm in arm with Jack, talking up a storm.

* * *

Fortunately for her peace of mind, Allie had several photo shoots scheduled during the ensuing days, and kept almost too busy to dwell on Jack and Michelle. Except in the evenings. She wondered what he was doing and if Michelle was still keeping him company. He deserved some fun after the horrors of war. And Michelle was young and pretty, and whole. She didn't walk with a limp or have to have a cane.

And as a nurse, she'd be very aware of his limitations, of the PT needed to bring his range of motion back as far as it could come. She'd be a help to him in many ways.

Allie would change the thoughts in her head to keep from dwelling on Jack, but they kept returning.

* * *

Thursday, she arose with anticipation. She'd spend several hours in Jack's company on the drive to and from Portland. They'd have lunch together before visiting the hospital and, if they stayed late enough, she might get to have dinner with him as well.

She wore her prettiest green blouse which highlighted her eyes. And the jeans she wore were new and fit perfectly. She shook her head at her reflection as she got ready. Not that he was likely to notice her jeans or even her blouse. He would focus on her limp, her cane and the fact she wasn't as outgoing and vivacious as Michelle.

For a moment she wondered if he'd invited Michelle to go with them. She could get an idea of what the hospital was like and maybe pick up an application form while they were there. It wasn't that Allie didn't want Michelle to get a good job, but she was hoping for today to be just her and Jack.

* * *

Able scooted up the ramp Jack set up and settled himself in the back of the SUV. He rested his head on the seat back and gazed at Allie. From the way his body moved, she knew he was wagging his tail.

Jack got in and closed the door. In moments they were off.

"Did the weather interfere with your picture taking?" he asked. The last several days had seen more rain than the entire time he'd been living in Rocky Point.

"We moved one venue inside. I was doing photographs for the paper--the sports section. So I was taking photos of all the kids on the various teams so they can run a special edition right before Thanksgiving. Instead of outside on the football field, everyone was inside the gym. And I had a formal setting of an engaged couple: Tate and Faith. You met him at the track."

"He's the Sheriff and she's the nurse."

"Ummm. Speaking of nurses, how is Michelle?"

"Still looking for work. She stopped by yesterday, but didn't stay long."

"I thought she might come today," she murmured.

"What?"

"Sorry." She repeated her statement in a louder voice so he could hear.

"Why?"

"In case she wanted to see the hospital and pick up an application, or something."

"That wouldn't take long. We'll be there for several hours."

She almost suggested the men there would welcome a pretty woman joining them to spend the afternoon. However, if Jack didn't think of that himself, she wasn't going to put the idea in his head.

The trip sped by and, before long, they ate lunch and arrived at the hospital. More men were in the community room than last time and called greetings, especially to Able. The dog pranced proudly by Jack's side, going up to each man and letting them pet him. With his eyes half closed, Able looked as if he could almost purr he was so content.

Allie went to sit with her usual group, but watched Jack as he spent time with each man, talking, assisting those who needed help with the tennis ball so they could roll it for Able. Her heart warmed and she gave a short prayer of thanks to the Lord for showing her it. Maybe this was what Jack should consider doing. His visits were bringing a lot to the men still in hospital. Some of them weren't ever going to be able to live on their own. Having one of their fellow soldiers come and spend time with them was special.

They stayed until almost dark and then reluctantly left.

"Did you see Josh Allarood? He actually rolled the ball for Able," Jack said when they were in the car.

"So did a lot of men," she replied, wondering why he'd selected this one to mention.

"But he's been almost catatonic in the months he's been here. He still didn't speak, but today he petted Able, and then took the ball when I handed it to him and leaned over and rolled it across the room. I think I saw the hint of a smile on his face."

"Fantastic! I'm so sorry I missed it," she said, glancing at Jack. "How did that make you feel?"

"Fantastic." He looked at her, their gaze caught and held a split second before she looked back at the road.

"I've heard of therapy dogs going into rest homes and convalescent hospitals to give patients a chance to pet them and be something out of the ordinary. You should see if you can get Able certified and then take him. There's an old folks home on the edge of town where I bet he'd be a hit. And a children's hospital in Portland. They'd really love him."

"I don't think so," Jack said, looking out the side window.

Allie wasn't sure what had been so threatening about her suggestions, but Jack seemed to instantly withdraw.

Help me, please, Lord. Let me say the right things to help him, she prayed silently.

"Do you want to stop for dinner on the way home?" she asked.

"No, let's get Able home. I didn't bring him any food and don't want him to have to wait any longer than he needs to eat."

They drove in silence until they reached Rocky Point. When she turned on Jack's road, he said stiffly, "Want to have pizza or something?"

Allie's heart blossomed. "I'd love to."

"We can order it when we reach my place," he said, relief evident.

Had he feared she wouldn't want to eat with him? She thought his refusal to stop for dinner meant he didn't want to extend their time together. Maybe he had been concerned for his dog, as he'd said.

It was still damp and cold after the rain. Indian summer had ended and the beginning of winter was moving in. His house was warm and cozy when they entered. Once the pizza had been ordered and Able fed, Jack struggled to get wood in the fireplace and started a fire.

"This is the best part of this house. I love having a fireplace," he said. "I've had a fire every night this week."

"I miss that at my place. My folks have one, but I'm in an apartment over a garage and there's no fireplace there," she said, sitting on the sofa which faced the blaze. She could already feel the warmth heating the room.

Jack sat beside her on the sofa stretching out his legs, cradling his right arm against his chest.

"You doing okay?" she asked, looking at his arm.

"Achy in this weather," he said, his gaze on the fire.

"Did you have a fireplace growing up?" she asked.

"At one place. We would do our homework in front of it in winter. It was more for show than providing warmth as the house had central heat. But my foster mom loved it. Didn't stay there but two winters." He trailed off, apparently lost in thought.

Jack watched the dancing flames. He had liked that family, that home. But when the man had been transferred, the social service worker would not let him leave the county, so he'd had to go to yet another home.

A nomad. That's all he'd been, was likely to be all he'd ever be.

"A penny for your thoughts," Allie said softly. Sometimes he had trouble hearing her.

"Just thinking what a nomadic life I've led. I think two or three years was the longest I ever lived anywhere."

"What was it like, being in foster care?"

"Okay, I guess."

"You moved around a lot?"

"Yes, foster parents are not adopting kids. They take them when they can. But if new babies are born, or men get transferred or someone gets an illness, they opt out and the kids are moved to a new home."

"That must have been hard."

"The settling in is. And the changing of schools all the time. It would have worked better if I could have at least stayed in the same school." He remembered the difficulties he'd had making friends if he was moved mid school year. All friendships had been established and he was odd man out for a long time. Like he felt here in Rocky Point.

"At least here, you can stay as long as you like, and make friends to last a lifetime," Allie said.

He looked at her, seeing a woman who had gone through hard times and still radiated optimism. He wanted some of that.

"Or not," she said a moment later. "Aren't you planning to stay in Rocky Point?"

Jack shrugged. "Too early to tell. It's a start for now, but I don't know how long before I'll think it's time to move on."

"And where would you move?" she asked.

He had no idea. In the army, he'd moved every two to

three years, or sooner when deployed. He'd envisioned being in the Army until he retired. Funny, he'd never thought of what he'd do once he was no longer able to serve.

He glanced at Allie noting the worried look on her face. Did she care if he moved away? At the moment he couldn't imagine any other place he'd rather be.

"No place special," he said.

She smiled, and he felt it like a blow to his heart. She was so pretty when she smiled, he wished she'd do it all the time.

"Then this is as good a place as any to make your stand. Settle down," she said.

"And do what?"

"Visit hospitals with your dog. Make friends. Maybe get married and have kids."

He couldn't picture himself married, much less with children. He could barely take care of himself, how could he support a family? He glanced at Allie.

"If that's so easily accomplished, how come you aren't married with kids?"

"Never met the right man."

"Never?"

She gazed into the fire for a moment. "Once upon a time I thought I'd marry Jason. We loved each other and had made plans for the future. Teenage dreams, I think. After he was killed, I thought I wanted nothing to do with anyone else. It hurts when someone you love dies. Gradually over the years, what I felt for him has become a really fond memory. I miss him. And the others on the minivan. I don't pine for him, however."

"Still not married."

She flashed him a smile. "If it's God's will, marriage will come. It could be I'm to be an example to others that I can have a happy life without marriage and family. It's not like I don't date. Just not a lot."

He couldn't see it. She was pretty and talented. She had a loving heart—he knew that from her visits to the hospital, from her concern for George and even Jason's mother. He could imagine her in the midst of excited children, all vying to tell her all about their day.

He couldn't envision a husband, however. Would he be someone from Rocky Point, or some soldier she'd meet at the hospital one day? One whose stay was temporary and who would be fully recovered in no time. Healed and able to take on a family.

He massaged his right arm again. It was gaining strength with the exercises he practiced faithfully. It would never match his left arm in range of motion, or ability, or strength. Still, he pushed himself to recover as much as he could.

Able sat up and barked, running to the door. A moment later, Jack rose and went to the door. "Pizza's here," he said, opening it.

Able ran to the edge of the porch, still barking.

"No," Jack said. The dog looked back at him and stopped barking. He sat and stared at the kid who got out of the car with the pizza box. The rain had returned and its drizzle dropped the temperature even lower. He was glad they had come home for dinner. And that Allie had stayed.

In moments they were sitting at the small dining table putting pieces of pizza on paper plates. It was cozy in the large house, and Allie wondered what the place would be like full of a family with lots of kids living in it. There were plenty of bedrooms for a large family.

"I wish the house could tell us who all lived here over the years," she said.

"It had to be a large family, don't you think? There are five bedrooms, three baths, two up and one down. And the kitchen is huge," Jack said, tackling the pizza.

The delicious blend of spices and tomato sauce was delicious. Allie had a thought.

"You know there's a Veteran's Day parade down Main Street on November eleventh," Allie said. "You could ride in one of the lead cars. It's to honor all veterans. You'd be perfect."

Jack looked horrified. "No way!"

"Why not? You're a veteran. You've served in a foreign war. You could join the American Legion and VFW."

"Not my thing."

"What is your thing?"

He met her eyes, "Serving my country, which is no longer an option."

"So find new options," she snapped. "You're not the only one in the world who got sidetracked from the original plan for your life. Are you just going to wallow in pity all the rest of the days you have?" She dumped her napkin on her plate and rose. "Thanks for dinner. I'm leaving."

"Wait."

"Nope, I'm done. I stupidly thought you wanted help in joining in the community. Obviously I misread everything. Call me if you want to join the human race again." She hurried to the door.

Chapter Six

Jack felt as if he'd been poleaxed. She was already at the door before he rose to go after her. By the time he reached the door, she'd dashed down the steps and into the rain. "Allie, come back."

She got in her car and, in seconds, was gone.

Able came to the top of the steps, whining.

"Yeah, I made a good impression, all right. Blast it!" He hit the post, wincing at the pain in his hand.

Staring out into the dark, Jack heard the echo of her words. He was not wallowing in pity. He was a fighting man. A man who faced reality. What could he do with the limitations he now had? He couldn't hold a gun. Couldn't defend himself in hand to hand combat. Couldn't hold down a job.

Couldn't--

He stopped listing all he couldn't do. She was right. He was wallowing in pity for all he'd lost. The Army had been his entire life. He felt adrift, uncertain about anything. The lodestone he'd followed had vanished. He'd had to reinvent who he was and what he could do.

He didn't want to. He wanted his old life back. A life he'd been sure of.

Able whined again.

"Go," Jack said. He was not going to accompany the dog on a night like this. He could do his business and get back in the house on his own. The dog took off down the ramp. In seconds he was lost from view.

Looking into the Stygian gloom, Jack felt he was looking into his future: nothing.

It was cold and damp. His arm and leg ached. Still he stood, waiting for Able. Waiting for some kind of revelation.

* * *

Allie drove through the drizzle trying to get her anger under control. She should not have lashed out at him like that. She was supposed to be encouraging him, not lambasting him for what she perceived as wrong. She needed to be supportive, not critical. Who was she to know what he was going through?

Actually, she was probably the best person in town to do just that. Hadn't she gone through the same thing ten years ago?

When she reached her driveway, she decided she didn't want to be alone with her thoughts. Calling Rachel, she was delighted when her friend answered.

"Want to go for some ice cream?" Allie asked.

"Out in the rain at this time of night?" Rachel questioned.

"I'm already out, so can swing by to pick you up. And it's not late, not even eight."

"Which is a good thing as the ice cream parlor closes at eight. I'll brave the rain for you. Something must be up."

"I need a double hot fudge sundae."

"Whoa, girl, something major's up. I'll be outside by the time you get here."

Rachel was standing beneath an umbrella at the walkway to her apartment building when Allie drove up. She hopped in and shook the umbrella, before collapsing it and bringing it to the floor of the car.

"So what's up?" she asked.

"I did something really stupid and need something sweet and decadent to recover."

Rachel laughed. "Tell all."

"It was Jack."

"Umm," her friend said.

"I yelled at him for being negative, depressed and self-pitying. I should know better. I do know better. But he's so wrapped up in what he can't do any longer, he's not seeing what he can do. He's incredible. He survived an IED, months of surgeries and rehab and now is on his own—something a lot of other men at the VA hospital will never attain."

"Cut him some slack, Allie. He's still newly recovering. He's what, almost thirty? So for twenty-eight or nine years he's had one mind set, now he has to revamp everything in his life."

"I know. That's what makes my outburst so bad. Plus, I know from my own experience that a person doesn't just change overnight. So why did I yell at him? I mean, he frustrates me. But I can deal with that. I just want the best for him. And I want it right now!"

Rachel burst out laughing. "Ever patient, that's our girl."

They parked in front of the ice cream shop on Main Street. It was practically deserted except for three high school girls giggling over something on one of their phones.

Allie ordered her double hot fudge sundae, while Rachel chose a more sedate single scoop of Rocky Road. They took the table the farthest from the teenagers.

"I think you're caught up with this guy," Rachel said when they were both seated.

"How do you mean?"

"More interested in him than I've seen you with others. He's special to you. And, as such, you want the best for him. But honey, your best may not match his best. He's still new to his limitations, a stranger in town, a lack of focus for a career. There's a lot going against him."

"He blames God, too, for the death of his friends and his injuries."

Rachel nodded. "I guess that's not unexpected."

"God's there to help us. We turn to Him when we need a stronger presence than our own. I can't imagine my life without the Lord in it."

"You've had a relationship with Christ since you were a girl. Jack might not have that kind of relationship yet."

"I invited him to the Veterans Day parade, that's what brought it up," Allie said slowly as she savored her dessert. She hadn't had that much pizza, so this was really dinner.

"I guess he said no."

"Right."

"I still say give him some time."

Allie shrugged. "He can have all the time he wants. I don't need to see him ever again."

Rachel looked surprised. "Hey, don't get all prissy. He needs friends. He needs a welcome into the community, to feel included. He'll forever be on the outside otherwise."

"If he wants to join in, he's a big boy; he can just join in," Allie said petulantly.

"What's the real story here," Rachel asked a minute later.

"What do you mean, that's the real story."

"No, it's not. You're upset about more than just his refusal to attend a parade."

"That's all."

"Stubborn," Rachel said with a teasing smile. "Did you go to the VA today?"

"Yes, with Jack. And I suggested he consider getting Able trained as a therapy dog and he about bit my head off."

"Not high on the idea, huh?"

"I think they'd be an awesome combination—especially at the children's ward of a hospital. You should see them with the men at the VA. Jack even commented that one guy did more today than he'd ever seen before because of Able. How can he not want to help fellow soldiers?"

"I don't know. Did you ask him?"

Allie shook her head. She finished the last of the ice cream sundae. "That was good." She looked toward the counter.

"No, one a night is enough," Rachel said.

Allie sighed. "I know, but a chocolate high can go a long

way to making me feel better."

"Until tomorrow, when you'll be complaining about all the calories you inhaled tonight."

"I did eat it fast, didn't I? Therapy."

"Umm." Rachel finished hers and looked out the window. "The rain's not stopping. Time to go?"

"Yeah, thanks for coming out with me. I feel better now."

Rachel nodded as she stood. "Give him another chance, Allie," she said softly.

"Yeah, I guess." She was disappointed, but her natural optimism would surely win out. Sometimes she wished she didn't have that streak.

* * *

It rained the next two days. Allie had a full schedule Friday and spent Saturday cleaning her apartment from top to bottom. Sunday after church, she went home with her parents and spent the afternoon with them.

Monday, the sun finally came out, but Indian summer was definitely over as the temperature remained cold. She wore a jacket and treated herself to lunch at Marcie's. She waved to friends as she entered. Marcie was not in the restaurant, but Allie saw Faith studying a menu and walked over.

"Want company?" she asked.

Faith looked up. "That'd be great. I don't know why I'm looking at the menu, I know I want the shrimp po'boy. I get that almost every time I have lunch here."

"That sounds good. It's my favorite, too."

When the orders were taken, Faith smiled at her. "So what have you been up to? Taken any fantastic pictures lately?"

"I've been to Shelley's to take photos of the baby. She's decided she wants one a month for the first couple of years since they change so quickly, and plans to have the same teddy bear in each so everyone can see how big little Amy is growing in comparison to the bear."

"Cute idea, and clothes for little girls are so adorable. We love the pictures you did for us. The newspaper ran with one, did you see it?"

"I did. You two are very photogenic. Did Tate's parents like them?"

"Of course. They're so wonderful. I'm really getting a terrific family, more than just Tate himself, which is pretty fantastic to begin with. You know I don't have family of my own."

"No, I didn't know that," Allie was startled to hear that.

"Raised in foster homes."

"Like Jack."

"Was Jack raised in foster care?" Faith asked.

Allie nodded. "The Army's been his life and family since he graduated from school, and now he doesn't have that."

Faith thought about it for a moment. "He needs something to do."

Allie laughed. "That's what I've been telling him." Briefly she recounted to Faith the visits to the VA with Able. "So I think he should think about getting him trained as a therapy dog and then take him to visit convalescent hospitals, the guys at the VA and children wards. There would be a lot he could do that would have such positive results."

"How does he feel about that?" Faith asked watching Allie intently.

"A flat no to my suggestions."

Faith nodded. "He's not comfortable outside the Army. I picked up on that when he checked in at the clinic. If he makes friends here, he'll feel more like he fits in and then may be open to new ideas."

"Only, he's practically a hermit and how can he make friends if he never goes anywhere?"

"He was at George's party."

"I tried to get him interested in the Veteran's Day Parade—another flat no."

Faith smiled at that. "Most men don't want to bother—until they get to be George's age, then they're proud of what they've done. Still, not many veterans in town. Maybe we could get all of them to participate and then Jack would fit in."

"Maybe."

Their sandwiches were delivered and the conversation veered onto different topics.

Allie wanted more for Jack than he seemed to want for himself. She didn't know how to do any more than she had done, however, so resigned herself to letting him fend for himself. She had her own life to live.

It was too bad she wanted to include him as part of that life.

The thought stuck. She did want to include him. To spend free time with him. To feel that delicious sense of anticipation when she knew she was going to see him. To laugh with him, throw the ball for his dog, and sit in front of a roaring fire again—just the two of them.

"Earth to Allie," Faith said.

"What? Oh, sorry. I zoned out for a moment. How's your dog?"

"She's doing great. Tate even takes her into work with him some times. Wish I could. I hear Able's cast will come off soon. I bet he'll be a happy fellow when that happens."

"It doesn't seem to hold him back much." She missed seeing the dog. And she missed Jack.

* * *

He slung a damp dish rag across the edge of the sink to dry. Daily chores were completed. Jack glanced at the clock. He'd finished earlier today than other days. A quiet sense of satisfaction filled him. He'd dusted, picked up and thrown the ball for Able. When not using the tennis ball for the dog, he constantly squeezed and released in his right hand. The fact he could even hold the ball and squeeze was a step up from a few months ago. The doctor had told him to be patient, give it time.

That was about all he had these days.

Able barked and ran to the front door.

The house was at the end of the street. The only thing beyond was the cliff and the sea. Was someone out for a hike? The dampness caused every bone in his body to ache. But the sun was shining at last and that was something. Too bad the warm weather had vanished with the rain. It was cold outside.

Jack walked to the living room and looked out the window. Able was dancing and barking and jumping up on the door as if he wanted to plow his way through it.

A sheriff's car pulled into his driveway. A moment later Jack recognized Tate Johnson as he got out.

What was the Sheriff doing here?

Jack went to the door and opened it as Tate walked up to the porch. Able dashed out, stopping when he got to Tate, sniffing, his tail wagging furiously.

"Sheriff," Jack said in greeting.

"Jack." Tate reached down to scratch behind Able's ears.

Jack glanced around. The sea was iron gray with frothy white caps blowing in the wind. The sparse grass struggling to grow was almost bent over with the strength of the wind.

"Come on in. It's cold out here," Jack said. He snapped his fingers and Able turned and trotted back into the house, going to sit beside Jack, his tail a lazy brush against the floor. "What can I do for you?"

Tate climbed the shallow stairs, taking off his hat as he stepped inside. "I was in the neighborhood and thought I'd stop by."

That didn't make sense. There was no neighborhood. The house Jack rented was a good half mile from the nearest house. Mostly there was only land and sea around the house. He shut the door.

"Get you something?" he asked, still standing by the door.

"Naw, I'm good." Tate looked around, stepped into the living room. "Nicer inside than out," he commented.

Jack shrugged. "It suits me."

"A bit large for a single man, isn't it?" Tate asked, walking across to the fire place, then turned with his back to it and looked at Jack.

"Can't beat the rent, though," he said. He was curious as to the Sheriff's visit. Maybe the guy liked to check out new residents to Rocky Point. They'd only talked briefly at the track that day.

"Have a seat," Jack said, sitting on one chair. Able lay down at his feet, his gaze firmly on Tate.

The Sheriff shed his jacket, tossed it across the back of another chair and sat on the sofa.

"How're you liking Rocky Point?" he asked.

"Fine."

Tate nodded, smiling at the dog. "My fiancee has a dog. I take her some days so she doesn't have to spend so much time in the apartment. They're good company."

Jack nodded. "This isn't my dog, though. It's really Allie's. I'm just keeping him until the cast comes off."

Tate raised an eyebrow. "Able might view that differently. He's sticking right by you. Border collies are defensive around their owners."

Jack leaned forward and gave Able a pet. "He'll guard Allie well," he said.

"No one's reported him missing. The vet said he hadn't

heard anything either. I don't understand people turning a dog loose like that. They should take them to a shelter rather than expect them to fend for themselves," Tate said. "He seems well mannered. Can you tell if he's had any training? If not, I can recommend the woman we use for Faith's dog."

Jack nodded. "That's an idea. I've taken him up to the VA hospital and he's really popular with the men."

"I bet they don't get to see dogs that much. Good job. I've heard of therapy dogs. They help out at hospitals and convalescent hospitals. Ever think of trying him on that?"

Jack shook his head, narrowing his eyes. "No, but Allie suggested the same thing."

Tate nodded. "Probably because it's a good idea."

Jack laughed. "Because it's your idea?"

Tate nodded, his gaze assessing. "Have you found a church family yet?"

That took Jack aback. Slowly he shook his head. "I'm not much on God these days."

"Oh?"

Wasn't it obvious? "I keep thinking about the men in the platoon that got killed. All the men getting killed, or maimed in war. What kind of God lets that happen?"

"We don't know all the ways of God. But I trust in Him and know He's in control. We may never know in this lifetime why certain things happen. I was married before. Did you know that?"

Jack shook his head.

"She died of cancer. It was hard. I swore I'd never let myself get that close to anyone again. But I did. I'm very much in love with my fiancee and can't wait until we get married. And you know what--she's a cancer survivor. Don't know yet how that's all going to play out, but I'm putting my faith in the Lord and letting things go the way He has planned. I'm happier than ever."

"How did you reconcile losing your wife?" Jack asked.

"I'm not sure I'm reconciled with it. I know she's with the Lord, so that helps. And life goes on so I'm making the most of it while I'm here. Trusting God helps. Actually it's the most important part of my getting over her death and opening myself up to love again. Anyway," Tate rose. "We have several different Bible study groups Sunday morning. Some are men only or women only, others are both. You're bound to find one to suit you. Come on Sunday."

Jack rose and Able immediately sprang to his feet.

"Could I have a glass of water before I leave?" Tate asked, snagging his jacket and hat.

"Sure, kitchen's this way."

Jack stood on the porch in the wind watching the Sheriff back around and with a wave drive off a few minutes later.

"Was that just about an invitation to church?" Jack asked his dog.

Able wagged his tail, looking up at Jack, a tennis ball in his mouth.

"Man, don't you ever get tired of fetch?" He took the ball and threw it across the lawn, quietly pleased with the distance. His right arm was definitely improving. Able raced after it, keeping his injured foot elevated.

"And how you do that is amazing," Jack murmured.

Rocky Point was a friendly place. And all the people he met seemed to center around the big church seen from Main Street. The birthday party had been there. What else was the place used for?

A couple of the foster families he'd lived with had attended church. He'd thought he had a good relationship with the Lord a few years ago. But his faith had faltered when faced with the horrors of war, with the death of his buddies.

He'd felt alone, adrift. Maybe he needed to rethink things. Reconsider priorities. Try to come to an understanding that man wasn't supposed to think like God. He was supposed to trust in Him and let Him lead.

How could he, though, when he thought about Ham and Rosco, and the guys at the VA and--

The dog ran back. His life was uncomplicated. He didn't show any signs of missing whoever had owned him before. He was happy to be with Jack. Able took each day as it came. Maybe he could learn from a dog.

"Come on, boy. I'll get my jacket and we'll take a walk along the bluff."

The wind was steady from the sea. The air tangy with salt. Cold though it was, once Jack began walking he relished the clean feel of the air. He'd have given almost anything to feel this in Afghanistan. The dry heat, the endless sand getting into everything, had had him fantasizing about snow storms and rain. He'd had the rain, now he had the cold. He was grateful for that.

Actually, he was grateful he was alive, he realized. Stopping in surprise, he looked out to sea, his gaze raising to the sky. The blue was so deep it almost looked indigo. The sun's warmth could be felt through his jacket.

"Thank you, God, that you spared me. Now what?"

As a prayer, he knew it wasn't much. Still, Jack felt a huge weight lift from him. Tears came and he blinked them away. He was alive, in his right mind, no PTSD. He was limited in what he could do compared to before, but he was alive. He was grateful for that.

Able barked and ran ahead, looking back at Jack.

"Okay, we'll walk. Thank you, Lord, for Able. I know I won't keep him, but he's just what I need right now. Something to focus on beside myself."

He frowned when he prayed that. Allie had gotten to him with her scathing words. He had focused on what he'd lost ever since the bomb. He should be focused on what he could still do. What he might be able to do in the future.

It wasn't much, but as a first step, for him, however, it was something amazing.

* * *

As Thursday approached, Jack wondered if Allie would ask him and Able to go with her to the VA. He could drive himself anytime, of course. But somehow he thought it better if the three of them went together. The question was, did she feel the same way?

He hated the fact she'd walked out the other night. And he had let her.

She'd been right.

Now he needed to tell her things had changed. Would she listen to him?

He took a breath. Only one way to find out.

The phone rang several times and then Allie's voice came on inviting him to leave a message.

He hung up. He wasn't going to leave a message. He wanted to talk to her.

"Want to go for a ride?" he asked the dog. He'd venture forth to town and see if he could see her on Main Street. That'd be good. If he saw her, he could get Able out of the car and have it seem as if they just bumped into each other.

"You're pathetic," he said to himself as he got the dog into the car. He'd faced down armed insurgents, fought through bullets, mortars and grenades. And now he was nervous about facing a pretty woman who barely came to his shoulder.

Rocky Point looked picture perfect when he drove down Main Street. It ran to the sea on a slight incline down to the water's edge where, to the right, there was a city park and, to the left, the road followed along the shore with warehouses and businesses side by side. In its heyday, Rocky Point had been a fishing and whaling port, and some of the old warehouses dated from the distant past as did many of the houses on the side streets.

Parking near the park, Jack put Able on his leash and walked through the grassy area to the sidewalk that led up the street. He scanned both sides, but didn't see anyone who looked like Allie. There were only a few people in sight. One walked briskly. A couple gazed in the large window of an antique shop. Three young women stood outside the ice cream store, talking and eating ice cream cones, not seeming to mind the cold.

He started up the sidewalk. He'd go to the top and come down the other side. Except for the time he'd come to the clinic, he hadn't spent any time in downtown Rocky Point. If anyone could call it a downtown. He could see the entire town from his vantage point. Nothing like Portland, or Boston and New York.

Yet a sense of peace started filling him. This was the picturesque town he'd envisioned when surreptitiously listening to Allie's stories at the VA. A sleepy New England town. Down a cross street he saw the church, clapboard painted white. Its steeple pointed to the sky. He could see a bell in the open place and wondered if it rang each Sunday to call people to worship.

When he reached the ladies eating ice cream, they all greeted him and made a fuss over Able. The dog loved it, his tail wagging a mile a minute.

"I'm finished with my ice cream, would he like to have the rest?" one of the women asked.

Jack had no idea if dogs were supposed to eat ice cream, but there was so little left in her cone he figured it wouldn't hurt. "I'm sure he'd love it."

And he did. When he finished, Able looked up at the other two ladies, eyes pleading.

They laughed, and each of them, handed over their almost finished ice cream for Able's enjoyment.

"He's going to be spoiled rotten," Jack murmured.

"He's so sweet. What's his name?"

"Able—for Able Company. He's really Allie's dog; I'm keeping him until the cast comes off."

"Then you're the soldier who has come to live in Rocky Point. I'm Evelyn Daniels," one of the women said, holding out her hand. "Welcome."

He looped the leash over his right hand, hoping Able wouldn't take in his head to run off and reached out his left.

"Oh," she said, somewhat flustered.

"It's okay," he responded. People never seemed to know how to take it. He was getting used to it and didn't want her to feel badly.

"I saw you at George's party," another said. "I'm Sara Longren. My husband works at the bank. And this is Betty Peterson."

"Ladies. Nice to meet you, I'm Jack Donner. Thanks for the ice cream. We had better be moving on."

Jack drew a deep breath as he took several steps further along the sidewalk. He wasn't good at small talk, but that had gone passably well. He hoped. Glancing in the windows of the shops and offices as he walked, he wondered if he'd ever feel like he belonged. He needed to make more of an effort to get to know the town and its residents. At least a few.

At the top of the hill sat Marcie's coffee shop. Through the wide windows, he saw several tables with customers, but no Allie. She was probably at home, or off on some assignment getting a green flash or some other kind of rare anomaly.

Able trotted along at his side, sniffing from time to time,

otherwise walking with his head held high. He was enjoying the outing. And, Jack realized, so was he.

He'd returned to the park and was about to go to the car when Able turned and began tugging on the leash.

Jack turned. Hurrying toward him was the very person he wanted to see. Allie had a big smile on her face and his heart turned over. He waited where they were—Able straining on the leash to greet her, his tail wagging furiously.

Allie looked as pretty as he'd ever seen her. She didn't hurry, but the smile never wavered as she walked straight toward him.

"Hi," she said when she was close enough. "I called, but I don't think you heard me. Good thing Able did."

She looked as if she'd forgotten about her scathing remarks the other night. He wanted to reach out and touch her. Feel her warmth. Hug her close and never let her go.

"I'm glad to see you and Able taking in Rocky Point. What do you think?" she asked. Her hair was blowing in the slight breeze, her eyes sparkled. He wanted to lean over and kiss her, feel her soft skin, have her undivided attention.

"Nice town, but I knew that coming here." He didn't want to tell her he'd been looking for her. He couldn't take his gaze from her. Maybe she'd guess.

"The park's nice. You can take him off the leash if you want, and if he won't run away," she said, leaning over to pet Able.

"Don't want to take the chance. We go for walks along the cliff, but there's not much to distract him there," Jack said, wishing he could think up some scintillating topic of conversation that would segue into what he wanted to tell her.

"I'll walk with you two for a little while," she said, tucking her hand in his arm. He clamped it close to his side.

"Were you on your way somewhere?" he asked.

"Nope, I came down to do some banking."

They walked into the park, following the path as it meandered among the trees. The grass was inviting and, after a few minutes, Jack thought he'd try Able off the leash. The dog raced around, always coming back to his side, then taking off again, barking at some seagulls that clustered near the far edge. The marina was clearly visible from the park—the boats bobbing on the water gleamed in the sunshine, washed clean by the recent rain.

"I'm going to the VA tomorrow. Want to go?" Allie asked.

He nodded. This was proving easier than he expected.

"Same time as last week, then," she said.

"Tate Johnston came to see me today," he said.

"Any particular reason."

"I'm not sure. I think to invite me to church."

Allie smiled at that, her eyes dancing. "We're united in wanting you at church. Sooner or later you'll have to give in and come, if only to get us off your back."

"Maybe I'll come this Sunday." There, that could lead into what he had to say.

"There's Sam Collier," Allie said, waving at a man just entering the park with his dog, a Beagle who was straining on his leash, wanting to be set free to run and meet the new dog in the park.

Sam unhooked his leash and the dog took off after Able. In only moments the two of them were sniffing each other, tails wagging.

"Looks like Able now has a friend in town, too," Allie said. "Hi Sam," she called when he walked closer.

"Hi Allie. Just the person I wanted to see. You know the Veteran's Day parade's coming up and we want to count on you to take the pictures."

"Already on my calendar. Sam, do you know Jack Donner? He's living at the Stafford place out the end of Water Street."

"Jack," Sam said, offering his hand. Jack took it with his left.

"Jack was a soldier in Afghanistan," Allie explained.

"Say, is that right? Just the man we need. How would you like to be our Grand Marshal this year? We asked George, but he said no. He's not sure he's up to it. Can't imagine a parade without George in it," Sam said.

Jack's initial response was no. Before he could say anything, Allie piped up. "What a great idea. Jack, you'd be perfect. And it's another chance for you to join in activities and let others in town get to know you."

He shook his head. "I'm not much for fanfare," he said.

"This is just a parade down Main Street at ten o'clock on Veteran's Day. Everyone comes out for it. The local DAR chapter hands out flags. Our Boy Scouts march with the colors. And the Veterans of Foreign Wars have a float. It'll be patriotic and fun. Say you'll do it. It gives everyone a chance to show appreciation for those who serve."

"Aren't there other vets in town? What about the VFW?" Jack remembered what Allie had said earlier.

"It's not really our VFW, but the chapter over in Pineville. But they come to our parade, because Pineville doesn't have a parade. And sometimes the National Guard sends a color guard. Maybe if you'll do this, we could get the other veterans in town to turn out, too."

"Put them all together in a car or on a float," Allie suggested. "George would come to that, I bet."

He couldn't say no to the excitement in her eyes, as she gripped his arm as she talked.

Yet he couldn't see himself leading any parade. He meant what he'd said: he wasn't much for fanfare.

"Don't say no just yet," Sam said. "Give it some thought. Here's my card. Let me know by Sunday, if that's okay. Or, I'll be at church if you want to catch me there."

Allie laughed softly. Jack glanced at her—knowing her thoughts. Did everyone in Rocky Point attend that church?

He took the card. "I'll think about it."

Able and the Beagle raced around the grass, barking and chasing each other.

"Your dog?" Sam asked.

"Temporarily," Jack said at the same time Allie said "Yes."

"How'd he hurt his leg?"

"Hit by a car."

"Gotta watch those dogs. This park's safe enough. Well, Bruno's had his exercise for the day. Got to get going. Nice to meet you, Jack. I hope you'll be our Grand Marshal this year."

"You could always have Able with you in the car," Allie said.

"What car?"

"One of the car dealers from Pineville always lets us have a convertible for the Grand Marshal. You'll sit up on the back and wave as it drives slowly down the street. Able would love it. Oh, do give him the opportunity. Think how proud he'll be."

He had to smile at that thought. The dog didn't care where he was, as long as he had a ball in his mouth or one to chase. It looked as if Allie didn't hold a grudge. Maybe he'd say yes, just to see her smile again.

* * *

When Allie and Jack arrived at the VA hospital on Thursday, Mason Albright, the hospital's administrator met them at the door.

"Got a minute, Jack?" he asked after greeting them both and giving Able a pat.

"Sure."

"Would you mind taking Able into the community room?" Mason asked Allie.

"Not at all. The guys are probably already waiting for him to show up." She held up a string bag with three clean tennis balls. "And for some serious throwing time."

"When the weather gets warm, I'd like them to play with

him on the grounds; get those who can manage some sun time," Mason said.

Jack glanced at Allie. Sounded as if the director already thought of their visits as permanent.

"What's up?" Jack asked, when they were in Mason's office.

"I have a proposition I wanted to make you. Ever thought about starting a halfway house for vets, who really don't need our facility but can't make it entirely on their own yet?"

Chapter Seven

J ack sat there, stunned at the suggestion. "Never crossed my mind," he said at last. "I can hardly take care of myself. I can't take care of anyone else."

"That's something I want you to think about. Your setup would be perfect, and Rocky Point sounds like just the place to see if this idea would work. We wouldn't release anyone who couldn't take care of himself. But maybe not all the way. At first it might just be one or two guys. Sam Pendarvis is good to go, except he couldn't take care of meals. You're cooking for yourself, right?"

At Jack's nod, he continued. "So add a bit more and make meals for two."

"Sam can't remember things," Jack said.

"Not everything. But he's doing okay day to day. Right now we don't believe he's going to get substantially better, but he's also no longer benefiting by being here. He has no family, has had no visitors since he's been here. He's like you, Jack. And I believe living on the outside would help. Not everyone agrees, but I've got the authority to try at least. What do you say?"

Allie's words echoed. *"You're not the only one in the world who got sidetracked from the original plan for your life. Are you just going to wallow in pity all the rest of the days you have?"*

An instant later, the idea that this was what God wanted flashed into his mind.

"There have to be lots of places around that would take a boarder," he said.

"Maybe, but you'll have a special empathy for him. You two have a bond that civilians will never understand. He needs this, and I think you need it, too."

"I don't know," Jack said slowly. He'd never thought about even having a roommate, much less one he'd be responsible for. It wasn't going to be easy. But he relished his release from the convalescent hospital, so wouldn't Sam?

"Think about it," Mason said.

Jack gave a half laugh. "I'm thinking about a lot of things these days."

"Oh?" Mason invited.

Jack spent the next few minutes talking about the parade, George, and Allie.

"You've got a good friend in her," Mason said.

"Yeah. That's all it can be," Jack said.

"Meaning?"

"Look at me, I'm a mess. I can't use my right hand, I'm half deaf—maybe more than half deaf—no stamina, no job, no prospects for the future."

Mason leaned back in his chair and studied Jack for a long moment. "You're thinking of marriage."

"I'm most definitely not thinking of marriage. It wouldn't be fair to saddle a women with my problems."

"You're not your limitations," Mason said firmly.

"Tell that to a prospective employer. If I'm so useful, why wouldn't the Army keep me on? There are desk jobs."

"Maybe because you're needed elsewhere. Think about this. I think it would be good for the men and for you."

"Don't I need some kind of red tape approval to do this? I don't even own the house. I'm renting."

"At this stage, it's experimental for us. A guy offers another guy a room. I've cleared it with the local doctor and Sheriff."

Jack narrowed his eyes. "Was that the reason for Tate's visit? To scope out my house?"

Mason shrugged. "I don't know about that, but he did give a glowing report on you, so whatever you've done, I'm impressed. You're well liked in Rocky Point."

That came as a surprise to Jack. "I hardly know anyone," he said.

"But those who know you like you. That says a lot. You've made a couple of good friends quickly. I'm hoping you can extend that to Sam, and maybe one or two others down the road. I'd also like you to continue bringing your dog here. I couldn't believe the change in Josh Allarood after being with the dog one afternoon. That alone makes me want to institute more interaction with pets. Too bad I can't get one permanently on staff."

Jack laughed. "Maybe a wounded K-9. Still Army. Why couldn't one of those dogs convalesce here?"

"Ummm, that's a thought." Mason nodded with a grin. "Can't you imagine the expressions on the faces of the general when I ask?"

Jack stopped in the doorway to the community room a short time later. Allie was sitting among several men, who were all laughing at something she'd just said. Able was across the room, dropping his ball in Josh's lap. Once again, the soldier who had been almost comatose was throwing the ball and outright laughing at the dog. What a difference.

"Hey, Jack, wondered when you were coming in," one of the men called. He crossed the room to greet him and the others, and was soon deep in conversation. A few minutes later, he singled out Sam. He had to decide if he wanted to try Mason's experiment.

* * *

When Allie pulled the car out of the parking lot a couple of hours later, she glanced at Jack. "Why did the director want to see you?" she asked.

Allie was the perfect person to kick around the idea with. She'd probably be able to point out all the problems he'd face living in Rocky Point.

So he told her.

"How do you feel about it?"

Dare he mention the feeling that had flashed through him in Mason's office? She'd immediately think it was fore-ordained.

"I said I'd think about it."

"Fine, but how do you feel about it?" she persisted.

"Almost as if it's meant to be," he replied truthfully.

"Ah, a God thing," she said, nodding her head as a smile lit her face.

"What?"

"When something is just perfect, yet out of the blue, I always think it's a God thing. He arranged for this to happen. I think would be good for both of you. Sam's a nice guy. He didn't deserve what happened to him any more than you did. So maybe this is the plan God had for your life all along."

"Couldn't He just have put the idea in my mind? Did everyone have to go through the hell of war to get to this point?"

"Maybe, but this way you have a special bond with anyone who comes to share the house. If you'd just thought up the idea and never had any hardship to compare, how effective would you be?"

He fisted his right hand, holding it as tightly as he could for as long as he could. Was it longer than the day before? He stretched out his arm carefully. It felt stiff, but it moved so much better than four months ago.

"Maybe you have a point. It's not like I'd be a caregiver or anything. I'd just provide a home and meals. I'm not sure about others managing the stairs, though."

"So they only recommend guys who can walk up and down stairs. It's just a start of an idea, and I think it's a great one. And if you need help, I know the members of the church would be glad to volunteer. George, for one, would urge them on in a heartbeat."

He nodded, feeling a tightness in his gut. Was he up to doing something like this? Would it lead anywhere? What if it flopped?

"So what doubts do you have?" she asked.

"A bunch. I'm not sure I'm the right person to try something like this."

"The director thinks so. And I like the fact the whole thing won't be tied up with a lot of red tape. Besides, if it doesn't work, you've tried and Sam would have had some time out of the VA hospital."

When Allie approached the last house on Water Street, she saw a familiar car.

"Were you expecting company?" she asked, as she pulled up behind Michelle's car in the driveway.

"It's Michelle. I wasn't expecting her, but she does drop in unannounced," Jack replied. Able stood up, his tail wagging. "Unless she just arrived, I'm curious why she waited; she couldn't know how long I'd be gone." He made no move to get out of the car, just stared at the front porch.

Michelle waved from where she sat bundled up in a thick jacket. Rising, she hurried down the steps and walked briskly to the car going around the front toward the passenger's side.

"I wondered where you were," she said, as Jack opened the door.

"We went up to Portland to the VA Hospital. Have you been here long?"

"Not long. I figured you'd be home soon. It's Able's dinner time. And I brought some dinner from Marcie's place." She leaned over a little and smiled at Allie. "Sorry, I only bought enough for two."

"Not a problem."

Jack got out and opened the back door, pulling out the

plank they were using as a ramp for Able. The dog danced down the wood and went to Michelle, tail wagging.

"Hey, boy, you're looking good," Michelle said. "Tell me all about your day," she said to Jack.

He leaned in the car for a moment. "Thanks for the ride," he said.

Allie nodded. Once the door was shut, she slowly backed out of the driveway, watching as Michelle took his arm and chatted as they walked to the porch.

It was disappointing that Jack and Michelle seemed to be doing more and more together. Not that she had any claim on him. But after the day they'd shared together, she would have loved to have him ask her to join him for dinner. Maybe talk about the director's idea, kick around different scenarios. She would encourage the idea, see if that was something that could satisfy his need to be independent and have plans for the future.

Instead, she was heading to an empty apartment and a solo dinner. Would Jack tell Michelle about the director's idea? Would he be making a decision with Michelle's help?

After a hasty dinner, she called Rachel.

"How'd your day go with Jack?" Rachel asked.

"Okay."

"Only okay? What happened?"

"Actually we had a nice enough day, but when I dropped him off at home, Michelle was there. She'd brought dinner—but only for two, as she was quick to let me know."

"Ah. Maybe you should have suggested dinner before taking him home," she said.

"I didn't think about it."

"I like Michelle and all, but this thing with you and Jack seems special. I'd sure let him know you're interested. Flirt a little. Invite him to your place for dinner. Take a picnic lunch."

"It's freezing out," Allie said. Yet the idea took hold. Maybe she could make dinner for them both. She bet Able would be able to get up the steps just fine. His cast was due to come off before too much longer.

"So maybe not a picnic this time of year. Do a dinner. Show him some of your pictures. Get him talking about his interests and see if you two have any in common," Rachel suggested.

"Matchmaker," Allie said wryly.

"You bet. He's a hunk. Why shouldn't he see the real you? Don't let someone else step in before you let him know you'd be interested yourself."

"Seems blatant."

"Absolutely. Faint heart and all that."

Allie considered what she could do within her own comfort level. "I could ask him for dinner. Spaghetti and the works?"

"Never knew a guy who didn't love spaghetti."

* * *

The next morning Allie booked two more appointments, happy to have the new work. She debated calling Jack or dropping by to invite him to dinner, finally settling on calling him. He accepted with alacrity which made her nervousness vanish. The rest of the morning seemed to fly by and shortly after lunch she went to the store to buy all the ingredients for dinner.

She'd make some more cupcakes, so he could take some home with him after dinner. Pushing her cart down one aisle, scanning the cake mixes, she looked up when she heard her name called. It was Harriet.

"Haven't seen you since Sunday," the older woman said.

"I've been keeping busy. How are you doing?"

"Getting by." It was her standard response since Jason died. She looked at the food in Allie's cart, a frown forming.

"Entertaining?" she asked.

Not that it was any of her business, Allie thought, but she shrugged. Remembering how hostile Harriet had been because of Jack at George's party, she didn't want to bring him up.

"I love spaghetti, don't you?"

"I do. Still a lot of food." Harriet looked at her sharply. "Inviting someone else over?"

Allie nodded. "A friend. I need to get going if I'm going to bake dessert. Nice to see you. Tell Paul hi for me." She pushed her cart, but before she could pass, the older woman stopped her by grabbing her arm.

"Who are you having over?"

"A friend, I said," she replied, irritated by Harriet's possessiveness.

"That soldier, I'm guessing."

Allie nodded. She wasn't going to deny it. Neither was

she going to put up with Harriet's interference in her life.

"What about Jason?"

"Harriet, Jason is dead. He died ten years ago. He was a special young man and we'll forever miss him."

"But you're moving on, right?"

"I'm living my life. Some days I feel I need to do that for Jason, and Wendy and Sara and Britta, and all the others who died that day. I don't know why I wasn't killed, but I feel I owe it to the others to live life to the fullest since they can't."

"You have a fine life."

"I want more." Startled Allie hadn't realized she even felt that way, much less able to blurt it out. "I want love, a husband, a family. I want grandchildren when I'm old, if I live to be old."

"Something I wanted, too," Harriet said bitterly. "Only I will never get them."

"So do you want me to go without because of that?" Allie challenged.

Harriet stared at her for a long moment, then dropped her gaze and released Allie's arm. Without saying another word, she pushed her own cart up the aisle and turned to the right.

"Whew," Allie murmured. She didn't think Harriet had thought things through. She and Jason had talked about marriage and a future with Doctors Without Borders. But it had only been talk. They had been too young to make definite plans. Life had not happened the way they'd planned. Harriet was sad and bitter over the loss of her only child, but Allie absolutely did not believe that, when all was said and done,

Harriet would want her to remain single all her life, denied the happiness of a solid marriage and a family.

However, if she did, Allie was not going along with that idea. For the first time since the crash, she was interested in a man who seemed slightly interested in her.

Maybe she was fooling herself and Jack's interest was solely because she'd been the first friend he'd had in Rocky Point. She hoped not.

Only time would tell.

* * *

By the time Allie heard Able's bark and paws on the steps, she was a nervous wreck. She'd made the cupcakes, had been simmering the sauce for hours. The noodles were ready to go into the pot and the garlic bread had started warming. Only the salad was left to fix. She had everything timed perfectly. Taking a deep breath, she went to open the door.

Able bound in, his tail wagging so hard his rear end moved back and forth. He came up and she petted him, lifting her gaze to the stairs where Jack was coming up. She caught her breath: he looked so strong and solid in the late afternoon sun.

"Hi," she said, smiling with happiness.

"Hi." He stepped inside and looked around.

Allie wondered what he'd think of her apartment. She liked lots of color and had reds, blues and cream as the main theme, with a splash of yellow here and there.

And pictures. Favorite photographs of shoots she'd

done over the years. One was a series of old buildings within driving distance; another a series of boats and the sea. Others were faces of children, family gatherings, formal graduation pictures and brides she'd known and photographed.

"Nice," he said, taking a deep breath. "Even smells great."

"I just have to cook the noodles and prepare the salad, and we can eat," she said closing the door behind him. "The kitchen's small, but would you like to join me there?"

"Sure."

Leading the way, Allie felt tongue-tied, breathless, on edge. "Able made it up the stairs fine, I see," she said, as the dog trotted along beside them.

"Didn't seem to have any trouble. I think he's about healed up. We'll know when we see the vet again."

The mundane talk about the dog helped ease her in to another topic and, before long, with the salad preparation to keep her hands busy, she relaxed enough to feel comfortable again with Jack.

It was odd to have him in her home. She loved her apartment, but tonight it seemed smaller than usual—due to his presence.

Jack perched on one of the stools she kept by the counter separating the kitchen from her living area. "What did you do today?" he asked, as she got the salad ingredients out of the refrigerator.

Briefly she told him.

He glanced over his shoulder to the living room. "Mind if I look at all the pictures you have up?"

"Go for it." Breathing space, that's what he'd given her. She had to stop this fluttery feeling. Maybe a moment or two alone while he looked at the pictures would help.

She watched him as she made the salad. Some photos he barely glanced at. Others he studied for several moments. She couldn't tell by his expression if he liked any of them. The black and white ones were a bit stark--the exact feeling she was aiming for. The wedding ones captured the romantic feel of the day. She did her best to minimize memories of the stress of a wedding, focusing on the happiness the couples shared.

The ones of the old buildings in the area seemed to hold him the longest.

When he returned to the kitchen, the salad was made, the noodles almost done. She'd set the table prior to his arrival, so that task was taken care of.

"You're really talented. I really can feel the history of some of the buildings. And feel bad for that derelict house. It needs to be taken in hand and returned to a place where a family could live," Jack said.

"I know. I used to fantasize about renovating it. It's not too far out of town, sitting near the cliffs and has a beautiful view. But it'd take a lot of money and work to bring it up to livable standards. It gets worse every year. One year, I expect it'll end up falling down from neglect."

Once seated at the table, Allie bowed her head. She offered a prayer of thanksgiving for the food and then smiled at Jack.

"I remember one of my foster mom's praying over each

meal," he said. "It's nice."

She nodded. "Maybe something you could do when Sam comes to share the house."

"If he does. Tell me about growing up in Rocky Point," he said.

"Haven't you heard a million stories at the VA?" she asked with a smile.

"Sure. But I could hear them again. I bet you were a cute little girl."

Allie laughed. "My mom and dad thought so." She remembered he had been raised in foster homes and didn't know whether to talk about family fun that he missed, or share it so he'd know what growing up in a loving home was like. She said a quick prayer for guidance and then began talking about her grandmother and how she'd taught Allie how to cook favorite recipes that had been in the family for years.

"I don't cook as much as I'd like. It's not that much fun for one," she finished.

"What's your favorite?" he asked.

"Oh, a sour cream pound cake that she always said would stay fresh and moist for at least a week. Only it never lasted that long in my house when we had it. My dad loves it and had a piece after every meal until it was gone. Even breakfast. I should have made one for tonight. I made cupcakes so you can take some home."

"Sounds good. You can make that cake another time and we'll share it."

She liked the sound of that and nodded.

"What's your favorite holiday?" Jack asked as they were finishing up.

"I love them all. My parents always made a big deal of each one. Maybe Christmas. I loved that one as a child. Now, I'm not sure. Maybe Easter for the message it gives. What's yours?"

"Fourth of July," he said without thinking about it.

"Not your birthday or Christmas?"

Jack shook his head. "I had some birthday parties, but because I moved several times, I didn't have the same friends year after year. Times were lean and so Christmas and birthdays weren't very different from regular days. But all of America celebrates July 4th. Parades, fireworks, picnics, the works. And in the military, it's celebrated as one of the most important holidays. I like that."

"Wait till you see Rocky Point's celebration. It's so much fun. Some folks have parties in their yard, and for those wanting to share in the community celebration, we go to Carlisle Beach for a huge potluck picnic and fireworks on the sand at night. You'll love it."

"I'll look forward to it," Jack said.

"I hope you're looking forward to leading the Veteran's Day Parade," she slipped in. He hadn't confirmed yet, but she was counting on him. "It'll be you and George and Connor Wentworth. Both of them said yes, if you'd do it. Unless it rains or snows, you'll get to ride in one of the convertibles Sullivan Automotive lends for the event."

He shook his head.

"I wish you would. It'll give everyone a contact to thank

you for your service, to show appreciation for our military. There are families here in town who can trace family back to before the Revolutionary War, and have had members participate in every war since. We love America as much as you do," she said. "Plus, think of Able. He could ride with you and have a red, white and blue bandana!"

He smiled at that, looking at the dog. "Want to lead a parade, Able?"

The dog leaped to his feet and wagged his tail.

"Guess that cinches it," Jack said, looking back at Allie.

"I'm so glad. I'll let the committee know. You'll love it, wait and see."

When they'd finished eating, Allie cleared the table, and brought out the cupcakes and a small dish of ice cream for each of them, including Able.

"Meals could be a problem," Jack said, carefully peeling off the wrapper from the cupcake. He carefully held it in his right hand, pleased it didn't tremble like it had before. He didn't have a lot of strength in the arm, but he had better control and range of motion. Maybe the doctors were right, he would recover even more mobility.

"Because?"

"I'm not much of a cook. Sam's not going to cook. He can't remember things very well and trusting him with something on the stove could be dangerous. We could be living on canned soup and steak on the grill."

"Not such a bad way to eat, but pretty boring after a while."

"Honey, after MREs, it's a feast." He dropped his gaze to

his cupcake and avoided her eyes. He hadn't meant for the endearment to slip out. She was the sweetest thing, but he had nothing to offer. No sense starting something he couldn't finish.

"That's the k-rations the military eats now, right?"

Thankfully she didn't appear to notice his slip.

He nodded. "Not a single one of them has chocolate cupcakes or vanilla ice cream in it."

She laughed. He could listen to her laugh forever. It was as sweet and joyful as she was.

"Guess it'd be hard to keep ice cream in the desert with no freezers around."

"Ummm." The moist cake was rich and flavorful. He glanced at her. Allie put a spoonful of ice cream in her mouth and slowly withdrew the spoon. The look on her face was enough to show the world how much she loved ice cream.

"I bet you frequent the ice cream store on Main Street a lot," he said.

She nodded. "Winter and summer and in between. I don't see why most people only like it in summer. It's always good."

"Try going without for a few years."

"Oh, that'll never happen. I need my fix too much to go even a few weeks without," she said with a laugh. "And it looks as if Able likes it, too."

The dog was licking around his mouth as if trying to get the last of the treat. His bowl was licked clean.

It was after ten when Jack said he should be going, and rose from the sofa where they'd been sitting. "Thanks for dinner and spending the evening with me."

"I've enjoyed myself more than I thought I would. Oops, that came out wrong," she said, rising as well and taking a step closer.

"Didn't you think you'd enjoy yourself?" Allie was so close, all he could do was think about what it would be like to kiss her.

"I was a bit nervous. I haven't had a man over for dinner since I got this place. I was worried about tripping and dumping the sauce over everything. Or being tongue-tied and at a loss for something to say."

He smiled. "Hard to believe you'd be tongue-tied."

She made a mock frown. "Does that mean I talk too much?"

He shook his head and stepped closer. "Not at all. Just right, I'd say."

He leaned closer and kissed her cheek, drawing in the sweet scent of her.

When he pulled back she was staring at him in surprise. Then she smiled and his heart lurched.

"That the best you can do?" she asked in a sassy tone.

He almost laughed. Did she feel this tug of awareness, this feeling of completeness when around him? He made the effort to cup her face in both hands, exhilarated his right hand responded. Her skin was so soft and warm. Slowly his eyes closed as he bent closer, until his lips touched hers and he kissed her like he'd been wanting to for weeks.

Allie moved closer and his arms moved to draw her right up against him while savoring the kiss. He could stay holding Allie forever.

Knocked from behind, he was startled and stopped the kiss, looking at Able who was wagging his tail.

"Guess we better go. I think he needs to use the yard and thought my getting up meant he was going outside." He didn't know what to say. He shouldn't have kissed her, but he couldn't resist.

Allie seemed less flustered than he felt.

"Not a problem. When he has to go, he has to go." She went to the door and opened it for the dog, then stepped outside as if to follow.

Jack felt the icy wind blowing in.

"Stay inside. We'll head out and there's no sense in your getting cold, or letting the warmth out."

"Okay." She reached out to touch his arm. "Thanks for coming. I'm glad you did."

"Thanks for inviting me." Some manners had rubbed off after all. He passed her and leaned in for another quick kiss.

"Come to church Sunday," she said. "Come with me and I'll introduce you around."

"I'll see." He should be saying no. He should be making his own way to Trinity Church, or taking Tate up on his offer to go with him.

But the thought of walking in with Allie had him dreaming of possibilities. Impossible possibilities.

Chapter Eight

Jack finished the last of the exercises his physical therapist insisted he do every day. He was breathing hard and a sheen of sweat covered his body. He mopped his face with his towel, using his right hand. He flexed the fingers and gripped the towel hard. Satisfaction filled him. He was improving. He would never be as strong in that arm as his left, but at least he could do more with it now than when he'd first been transported. His fear back then had been he'd lose the arm entirely.

A car sounded on the graveled driveway and Able went to the door, barking, his tail wagging.

Jack glanced out the window. It was Michelle. He debated not answering the door, but she had to know he was home. His car was in the driveway and the dog was barking. She knew he never went anywhere without Able.

Reluctantly he went to the door and opened it just as she ran up the stairs, a covered platter in her hand.

"Hi, good morning," she said with a beaming smile.

"'Morning." He made no further move of invitation, but Michelle didn't appear to realize that. She kept walking, until he moved out of her way before she bumped into him.

"I brought you a lemon meringue pie, made it myself. I thought you'd enjoy having some dessert later." She walked through to the kitchen.

He followed, slinging the towel around his neck. "Thanks."

She smiled at him. "Been exercising?"

He nodded, watching as she placed the pie on the counter, then noticed the cupcakes already pushed back so not to tempt Able.

"Oh, you already have some dessert," she said.

"Allie made them."

"How nice." She smiled and then turned. "I thought we could take a drive or something. It's pretty cold outside, but a lovely day otherwise. Have you been to Carlisle Beach? It's south of town. And no rocks—just a long stretch of sand. We have barbecues there in the summer. The water's pretty cold even in August, but it's fun to walk along the edge of the ocean. Able can come, too. I brought a towel to put on the back seat."

Before Jack could respond, the phone rang. He reached out to answer it, surprised to hear Tate Johnston on the other end.

"What can I do for you, Sheriff?"

"Jezzie called. She asked if I could bring you by to see George. He's worrying her and she thought between the two of us, we could find out what's bothering him. He won't talk to her about it."

"Sure. When?"

"I could swing by and pick you up in about fifteen minutes."

"I'll meet you there," Jack said, his gaze focusing on Michelle. He felt conflicted. He knew she was interested in him, but there was no future between them anymore than with Allie. Less, actually. He was attracted to Allie Turner in a way he'd never experienced before. Nothing like the early stages of friendship he had with Michelle. After last night, he was not in the mood for spending time with Michelle.

He hung up the phone. "Sorry, I'll have to take a rain check on the drive."

"I gathered that. What does the Sheriff need you to do?"

"Help out, if I can. I have to get a shower before I leave. Thanks again for the pie."

"Sure." Her smiled seemed a bit more forced, but she walked back to the front door, saying goodbye.

Once she was in her car, Jack hurried to the bathroom and a quick shower before going to George's. What could be upsetting the old soldier? He thought he and Jezzie were tight. What couldn't he tell her that Tate thought he'd tell the two of them?

"Thanks for coming, Jack," Jezzie greeted him at the door. Tate was already in the living room, talking with George.

"What's going on?" Jack asked.

"I don't know. He's been agitated for a couple of days now.

"Hey, George," Jack said, joining him and Tate.

"Jack. Tate said you'd be coming. This is foolishness. Jezzie shouldn't have called you," the old soldier grumbled.

Jack sat in the chair near the sofa. "She knew I'd want to help however I can. What's up?"

George looked at Tate and then Jack. "Nothing."

"So you always give Jezzie a hard time over nothing."

George seemed surprised, glancing over at his grand-daughter. "No hard time."

"Well, you have me worried and that's about the same thing," she said. "I've asked you a dozen times what's wrong and you won't tell me."

"Umph, so you think I'll open up to these two?" the old man grumbled.

"Soldier to soldier," Jack said.

George looked at him, narrowing his eyes. "Maybe you'd understand after all."

Everyone leaned just a bit forward as George cleared his throat.

"Foolishness," he muttered. He glared at Jezzie, then looked at Jack.

"Guy in my old unit died a few days back. He and me and Philip Harley are all that's left. The funeral will be at Arlington next week."

"Grandpa, I'm so sorry," Jezzie said, coming over to give him a hug.

"And you want to attend the funeral," Jack guessed.

George shrugged. "I know it's impossible. I can't get around like I used to. It's just--"

"So go," Jack said. He would have given anything to have been able to be at the funerals of the men in his unit who had died. He'd been in the hospital for weeks after the attack;

it'd been impossible to go. But he understood George's yearning. If they'd kept in touch all these years, there was a special bond there.

"Can't." George replied.

"Why not?"

Jezzie caught her bottom lip between her teeth, then said, "No way to get there and, once there, it's hard for him to get around. I can't take time off to take him. Right, Grandpa?"

"So I'll take you," Jack said. He'd have gone in an ambulance to Ham's funeral if someone had taken him. There was a special bond between men who served together. Death didn't sever that bond.

Everyone looked at him.

"Son, you can hardly get around on your own," George protested.

"I can drive, and we'll find someone at Arlington to push a wheelchair. What more do we need?"

"You sure you're up to that?" Tate asked.

"Like I said, we can drive, take a couple of days down and a couple back. If George wants to see his old friend laid to rest, I'm all for him going." He glanced at Jezzie. "If he's physically able."

"He still takes care of himself. But he tires easily and can't walk long distances."

"A wheelchair—I could get to the grave in that." Hope shone from his eyes.

"Do you have the specifics of the day and time? If so, I'll take care of the rest," Jack said.

"Son, you don't know what this means to me."

"Actually, I do."

George studied him for a moment then nodded once. "Guess you do at that. I'm obliged."

George got the letter Philip's family had sent him and handed it to Jack. "Tell me what time to be packed and I'll be ready."

"Why didn't you tell me?" Jezzie asked.

"Didn't want you to fret. Nothing you could have done."

She nodded. "Thanks, Jack. I appreciate this."

Tate and Jack left a short time later.

"Thanks, man. If I'd known what he wanted, I would have seen if someone could have driven him down to Arlington," Tate said as they stood by their cars.

"I'd rather do it. I have some friends myself I can say goodbye to," Jack said.

Tate nodded and turned to his car, then stopped and looked back. "We'll all pray for a safe trip for the two of you."

Jack nodded. Another reason to get to church.

Once home, he let Able out of the car. Instead of going inside, however, he turned toward the cliffs. A walk in the sunshine would give him time to think about all he'd need to do to get this trip underway. He'd surprised himself with the offer. The longer he thought about it, however, the surer he was that this was right. Pausing at land's end, he stared out over the blue Atlantic. Raising his eyes, he looked into the endless blue of the sky.

"Hey, God. I know Tate said they'd pray for us, but

maybe it's time I added my own prayer. Let George see his old friend laid to rest. Help him with closure. It's tough to lose comrades in arms. I know that. I still don't understand why you spared me and took the others. I'm grateful. So thanks."

He felt a peace spread through him.

Able nudged his hand.

"Okay, let's walk." They followed the edge of the cliff for more than a mile before turning back.

Once in the house, Jack called Allie.

"I have a favor to ask," he said after greeting her.

"What is it?"

"Can you watch Able for a few days? I'm heading to Washington, D.C. and a funeral at Arlington."

"Oh, no, did one of your friends die?"

"Not mine, an old friend of George's." He told her about his visit to the old veteran and his offer to drive him down to the cemetery."

"Are you up to it?" she asked.

"Tate asked the same thing. I'm fully capable of driving, taking care of myself. Might not be one hundred percent, but I'm not an invalid."

"No offense intended, just curious."

"Can you watch Able while I'm gone? I don't think this is a trip for him."

"Sure. Not a problem. At least he can take the stairs okay."

"Thanks. I'll bring him by on Sunday. We'll be leaving right after lunch."

"That'll be fine."

"Do you want to go to lunch with me after church?" he asked. He almost held his breath waiting for her response.

"I'd love to."

He let out his breath. Good.

The next few minutes were spent in contacting the hospital administrator for names of contacts in the D.C. area. By the time the afternoon was over, Jack had mapped out their trip, had someone lined up to help out at Arlington Cemetery, and started thinking about what he'd wear to the cemetery. He'd wear his uniform. He wondered if George still had his. Time would tell.

* * *

Sunday morning, Jack took Able for a walk, then packed up the dog's bed, his leash, bowls and food, loading them in his car for the drive to Allie's place. He packed his own things and stowed them in the trunk. Making sure the kitchen was clean and the place tidy, he headed for Allie's. Once lunch was over, it would be time to get George and make the first leg of their journey. He planned to reach Connecticut before dinner. He and George would spend the night there, and drive the rest of the way into Virginia on Monday. The funeral was Tuesday morning. They'd be back on the road by early afternoon to retrace their trip.

Allie met them when they arrived and helped carry the things into her apartment. Letting Able wander around, sniffing every bush and tree, she then put him in her apartment and they drove to church.

When they arrived at the clapboard building, the parking lot was filling up fast. Jack parked near the back. Turning off the engine, he reached into a pocket and held out a key.

"What's this?" Allie asked.

"Key to my place. I think I brought you enough food for Able, but if not, you can get more from my place. You don't need to buy more. I included two tennis balls in his bag, but if he loses them, there're a bunch in the cupboard over the stove."

"Over the stove?"

"As good a place as any when trying to keep them away from him. He'll take them all out and scatter them around the house, then go and round them up, making a neat stash usually right where I need to walk."

She laughed. "Enterprising dog," she said, as she tucked the key into her purse.

Entering the church a few minutes later, Jack was immediately the center of attention. Tate Johnson met him in the vestibule with Faith at his side.

"Glad you could join us, today, Jack. You already know Faith. Hi, Allie."

Greetings were exchanged, and then Rachel joined them. Before even entering the sanctuary, Jack was greeted by several people he'd met at the open house at the car track and at George's party. He nodded across the way to Nick Kincaid. He recognized Marcie from the café, standing close to the former Grand Prix racer. The man next to him had to be his brother, whom Jack hadn't met yet.

"Jack, I didn't know you were coming today." Michelle came from a side hallway and smiled. When she saw Allie beside him, her smiled faltered a little. "Oh, hi, Allie."

"Hi, Michelle."

Harriet and Paul entered behind them. When Allie turned to greet them, Harriet glared at Jack, then Allie. Ignoring her, she walked swiftly into the sanctuary.

"Whoa, what's wrong with Harriet?" Michelle asked.

Allie knew exactly what was wrong, but she wasn't going to spread that around. "Bad hair day?" she said.

Michelle shrugged. "See ya." She followed the Lodges into the sanctuary.

"Let's go in, the service will be starting soon," Allie said softly.

Jack made sure he sat on Allie's right, so he could hear her if she spoke to him during the service. He recognized some of the hymns and did his best to keep up. Sometimes he kept quiet and listened to the words as others sang. Memories from childhood played in his mind.

When had he stopped attending church? Why hadn't he gone since on his own?

Pastor John delivered a sermon on giving more than what was asked for. Jack listened, glad for the man's strong voice. He heard almost everything except when the congregation laughed at something. The message struck home. He'd given more. The men in his unit had given far more than they planned when signing up to serve their country. It had all been done willingly. He'd do it all over again in a heartbeat—even knowing the outcome.

He glanced at Allie as she watched the pastor deliver the message. She gave more than she needed to. When his gaze went across the aisle, he saw Mrs. Lodge's head bowed. She gave more—but in the wrong way. Her expectations and demands of Allie were uncalled for and petty. He knew how hard it was to lose someone to death. That didn't give her the right to try to wrap Allie up and keep her away from whatever life offered. The marriage between her and Harriet's son would never happen. That didn't mean Allie shouldn't find happiness.

Could she with him?

The thought startled him. He had nothing to offer. He'd look for work, but didn't expect to find much for a man with his limitations.

Still, whatever worked out would be fine by him. He slowly came around to letting the Lord decide. If He wanted him to have a sustaining career, He'd guide Jack in that direction.

Allie glanced at him and met his eyes, smiling. She was always smiling. It was one of the things he liked about being around her. She always seemed happy. He wanted that for himself.

* * *

Allie and Able waved Jack and George off shortly after a full lunch at Marcie's café.

"So it's you and me for a few days. Want to go for a walk?" she asked the dog.

He barked once and stood, ready to go.

She laughed "Okay, fine, but I need to change first."

As soon as they started their walk a little while later, Able headed toward the main part of town. They walked along Main Street, Able sniffing every lamppost and bench while Allie window shopped. Most of the stores were closed on Sundays, only a few opened at one o'clock for the tourist trade. This late in the year, it wasn't profitable to stay open all weekend. The summer months were different; then most of the stores opened after church.

When they reached the park, Allie took Able off the leash and let him run toward some ducks near the breakwater. He barked and chased them away. He kept his injured leg lifted, but it didn't seem to slow him down any. She sat on a bench and watched the dog run back and forth. Once he tired of that, she pulled a tennis ball from her pocket and sent it sailing over the grass.

Finally Allie decided Able looked a bit subdued, though not particularly tired out. He had enough energy to keep going fetching balls until dark. But she was getting a bit chilled sitting in the waning afternoon sun.

"Let's go home, boy," she called.

The apartment felt invitingly warm when they entered. She knew it was November, but it had been so nice a few weeks ago, it was hard to believe it was already getting to be winter. She called her mother to chat since they hadn't had their usual Sunday lunch together. When her mom had invited her for dinner, she declined. Without consciously thinking about it, she wanted to be home in case Jack called when he and George stopped this evening.

After dinner, she went out with Able. The stars had begun to shine and she looked up, wishing she knew more about each one. Getting cold a few minutes later, she called the dog.

No response. No brown and white dog racing across the yard.

"Able!" She tried to see in the darkened yard, but saw no movement.

"Able! Come!"

Several fruitless minutes later she hurried up the driveway to the road, calling him, stopping to listen for any sound that would indicate where the dog was.

She couldn't find him anywhere.

Looking up and down the road, she saw no sign.

"Where are you? Able!"

What was she going to do? She knew Jack let him out of the house and the dog always stayed close by. Would he have gone back to Jack's?"

She got in her car and traced the route to the house at the end of Water Street. When she slowly turned into the driveway, her headlights spotlighted Able, sitting on the front porch, panting. He must have run all the way.

"Able, what are you doing here?"

He wagged his tail and turned toward the door, barking.

"Jack's not home, boy. You're staying with me."

Able barked again, scratching once on the door.

"Come on, boy, you're staying with me." Allie snapped on the leash and led him back to the car. He came willingly.

She kept the leash on him until they were inside her apartment. She'd have to keep him on the leash whenever they were outside to keep him from running away.

Allie had not taken her coat off before the phone rang. She hoped it was Jack. Thankfully she had his dog safe.

"Hey," Jack said when she picked up.

"Hi. You made it to Connecticut?"

"Yep, safe and sound. We had dinner and then George decided to go to bed. We have adjoining rooms, so I'll check on him before I go to bed. We left the door open a crack. It was a long drive."

"I bet. Are you sure you should have undertaken this?"

"Yes, more sure after the discussion we had on the drive down. I feel a special bond with George and he understands me. It's all good, Allie."

"Well, your dog gave me a scare tonight." She proceeded to tell Jack about Able's escapade. He laughed.

"You need to remind him he's your dog," he said.

"Ummm, about that. I'm not sure that's going to work. I think Able thinks he's your dog."

"I can't have a dog," Jack said.

"What are you talking about, you do have a dog and he adores you."

"But the original deal was I'd keep him until he healed."

"I don't mind changing the deal, so you can keep the dog that loves you. I'll come to visit."

"Often, I hope."

Allie caught her lower lip in her teeth. She liked that comment.

"Sure." Her heart beat a bit faster.

"What did you do this afternoon?" he asked.

She settled in on the couch for a lengthy discussion. If he wasn't in a hurry to hang up, neither was she.

It was an hour later before Jack said he had to go. He promised to call the next evening to let her know how everything went, and what plans there would be for the funeral on Tuesday. Once they hung up, Allie rose and called the dog. One more quick trip outside, and it was bed time for both of them.

* * *

The next morning Allie took Able with her when she went to a preliminary meeting to discuss a wedding in Pineville she was shooting. The bride to be was delighted to have Able sit in on the planning. He lay right beside Allie as they met and gave no trouble. She praised him on their way back to Rocky Point.

"If it were summer, you could sit on the patio and I could eat out there with you. Marcie doesn't mind dogs as long as they are not inside. But it's too cold to eat out today. I'll make do with a homemade sandwich. She pretended it was a big deal and Able barked at her. Laughing, she glanced in the rearview mirror at the dog. "I think you really can understand me."

Reaching home, she opened the back door and pulled down the ramp. Before she had it in place, however, Able jumped from the rear of the car and ran up the driveway toward the road.

"Able, come back," Allie turned and called after the dog, but he was gone.

At least this time she had an idea where to find him. Reloading the ramp, she hurried to take off after the dog. This was not behavior to condone!

With no delay after he took off, she caught up with him before he turned onto Water Road. But when she stopped the car and called him, he ran right past her and kept on running, his cast held several inches off the road.

She arrived at the house before the dog, but only by a couple of minutes. When he came into view, he veered around the car and dashed up to the porch, barking at the door.

"All right. I have a key. Let's get you some water and have you check out the place. Jack is not here."

Able trotted right into the kitchen, looking for his water bowl. Allie got down one from the cupboard and filled it for him. When he finished drinking, he made a tour of the house. He came back to the living room where she sat waiting.

"I told you he wasn't home."

He looked at her a moment, then went back to the kitchen. A minute later she could hear him walking through the house again.

Able walked through twice more, then came to lie on the floor in front of Allie, the air whooshing out of him.

"I told you he isn't here. But if it'll make you easier, we'll stay a bit. You're probably homesick."

She got her notes from the car and sat at the dining table to plan out her part of the wedding. She could work just as well here as at home.

When it was time for dinner, Allie called Able and he came readily enough. She made sure she had a firm grip on the leash. Once back home with no mishap, she vowed to keep better control on Jack's dog until he returned home.

* * *

Allie stayed near the phone all day Tuesday hoping Jack would call. But the only calls were from clients. Wednesday, she was impatient to hear how the funeral had gone. She knew they were expected to drive back to Connecticut today and then be home sometime tomorrow, but not hearing made her anxious. What if they'd run into problems? Surely Jack would alert someone in town.

Not hearing from him had her doubting. Was he getting involved in their community, or was he merely marking time until he could move on as Harriet suggested? There was nothing compelling to hold him in Rocky Point. He had no lasting ties in town. Even the rent on the house was month to month. Maybe he ran into some friends in Washington. Would he want to relocate closer to those he'd known for years, rather than stay in a town where he was still a stranger?

Allie kept busy with work. Still the time dragged by.

Thursday afternoon, she took Able for a walk in town. The day was cold, the breeze from the sea brisk. But the park was bathed in sunshine and the dog loved running around and chasing the seagulls. She began to suspect the birds were enjoying the activities as much as the dog, as they kept returning.

Able turned and ran toward town. Allie rose, afraid he was heading home again. She didn't want him on Main Street. He wasn't used to the traffic. When she turned, she saw Michelle petting Able.

"Hi," she said, walking over. Maybe she should snap the leash back on the dog.

"Hi," Michelle said, looking around the park. "I saw Able and thought Jack would be here. I haven't seen him for a couple of days."

"He took George to Washington, D.C. They're expected back later today," Allie said. So Jack had not told Michelle where he was going. Interesting.

"Oh, that was nice of him. I wanted to tell him I got a job. It's at a hospital in Augusta."

"Good for you. I know Jack'll be glad to hear that," Allie said.

Michelle nodded, looking at Allie. "You're watching Able for him?"

"Yes. And this dog really misses him. He's run back to the house a couple of times. I was worried that's where he was heading when he saw you."

Michelle smiled brightly. "I had hoped Jack would want to celebrate with me, but if he's not home, I guess not. I have to get to Augusta tomorrow to check out apartments. I start work in a week, which doesn't give me a lot of time to find a place and move in."

"You'll have to come back after you start and let us know how the job's going," Allie said.

Michelle looked at her. "Us, hmmm." She sighed. "I guess I'll take off, then. Tell him I'll be in touch." She gave Able one last pat and then turned and began walking up the street.

Allie watched her, feeling a bit sorry for the woman. She obviously liked Jack a lot. And who could blame her; Allie like him a lot herself.

Had he kissed Michelle? She hoped not. She wanted their kisses to be special—just the two of them. She turned back to the park, wondering if she should make more of an effort with Jack. Michelle made no bones about being interested in the man. Allie was more than interested, she was halfway to falling in love with him.

The thought shocked her. She gazed at the sea as the realization sank in. She knew she felt more for him than anyone else. But was it love?

For a moment she tried to picture herself and Jack building a life together. It wasn't hard to do at all. Her heart raced, and the smile came without thought. She'd love to build a life with Jack Donner. But would he want to build one with her?

* * *

Jack pulled into the driveway and cut the engine. He leaned back and just sat there for a moment. The trip had been more than he'd imagined. A quiet sense of satisfaction filled him. He'd gone the distance. He'd handled every detail. And his stamina had not failed. The images of the last few days crowded his mind. He and George had enjoyed each other's company on the ride. He'd been filled with quiet pride at the funeral, knowing he'd given his best for his country. And he was glad he'd been able to get George there. The old soldier had ridden down and back to the grave in the wheelchair a young private from Fort Myers had pushed. But at the grave-side service, when they played Taps, he'd stood at attention as the others in uniform had done.

When all was said and done, the trip had been well worth it. Even though he was so tired now, he wondered if he could get out of the car and into the house.

He heard Able bark. He sat up and looked around. The dog was jumping up against the car, barking and carrying on. Jack looked around. He didn't see Allie's car. How did Able get here?

He opened the door and the dog jumped in his lap, licking his face, wiggling in his excitement.

"Hey, boy, what are you doing here? I'm glad to see you." Jack laughed at the dog's antics, finally getting him off so he could get out of the car. He still didn't see any sign of Allie.

"You're the welcoming committee?" he asked as he went to the trunk to get his bag.

Able barked again and ran to the porch, scratching at the door.

"Okay, I'm coming." Maybe there was something to having a dog. No one had ever greeted his return so joyfully. Actually, no one had ever been there when he'd returned from an assignment.

He had just stepped on the porch when he heard the car. Turning, he saw Allie pull in behind his car.

She got out of the car and hurried over. "That fool dog has come back here more times than I care to count! Able, you can't run off like that!"

Jack laughed. His heart filled with gladness at the sight of her.

She looked at him and smiled, dazzling him with the feelings that clamored inside.

"Welcome home," she said, and reached out to hug him. He hugged her back, holding her close, savoring the sweet scent of her, the joy that seemed to shine right out of her. "How was it?" she asked, still holding on to him. He could stay like this all day.

She pulled back. Reluctantly he let her go. "It went well. George was a hit. There were members of his friend's family there and they knew all about George. We had lunch together after the service. It was hard for him at times. I think it helped the family to talk about the old times he'd shared with his friend."

Allie pulled out her key and went to unlock the door. "I've brought this dog here to wander around. He didn't seem to believe you weren't here. Forget him coming to live with me when he's better. This has proved you are the one he wants."

She stepped inside and Jack followed. For a moment he had a feeling of homecoming.

"Okay, then," he said.

Allie whipped around and stared at him. "No argument?" she asked.

He shook his head. Was that the way she saw him—always arguing?

"Great, I know that'll make Able happy."

"Can you stay a while? We could order pizza again," he said. Then wondered if that was wise. The last time hadn't ended well.

"Sure. If you're not too tired from your trip."

"Not at all." Just being around her gave him energy.

"Tell me all about it," she said, as he went to stack some logs in the fireplace and get a fire going.

Jack sat on the sofa while the blaze began to heat the room. Allie sat beside him, turned slightly to face him. He told her of the trip down, of being at Arlington, and the return journey.

They ordered pizza and discussed what Allie had been doing while Jack was away.

"Oh, Michelle got a job in Augusta," she said at one point.

"Good." He was glad Michelle found a job—and that it was not in Rocky Point. He didn't know how to distance himself from her, but she wanted more from him than he wanted to give.

Unlike Allie. He wasn't sure where he stood with her. Today's welcome gave him hope.

To what end, he asked himself at one point in the afternoon. Today was proving he wanted the same things most men did—someone to care for them. To miss them when they were gone. To welcome them home.

His musing came to a crashing halt when he considered

what he had to offer. Very little.

* * *

Allie didn't want to leave, but she could tell Jack was getting tired. She debated leaving after dinner, but wanted to stay as long as she could. They moved back to the living room and sat in front of the fire.

"Did you go to the VA hospital today?" he asked.

"No. I called and said I'd go tomorrow. Want to go with me?"

He nodded, leaning his head back against the sofa. "I know the men would miss your visit if you didn't go," he said.

"I'd miss them. Tomorrow's supposed to be a sunny day, even though I doubt the temperature will be warm. We can take Able. The director especially asked for him when I called to say I'd be in tomorrow. I think they like his visits better than mine these days."

Allie looked at Jack when he didn't respond. He'd fallen asleep.

She smiled ruefully. So much for her scintillating conversation. The guy was wiped out from the trip. She should have left when they'd finished eating.

Allie rose and went to let Able out one more time. Once he was finished, she made sure the fire was safe, and went to hunt for a blanket to cover Jack. That done, she turned off all the lights but one lamp and let herself out of the house.

She'd see him again in the morning. She could hardly wait.

Chapter Nine

Jack awoke with Able's face in his. He blinked and looked around. The dog whined and ran to the door. It was morning. He sat up and shook his head. He'd obviously fallen asleep on the couch last night. Then he remembered and almost groaned. Some host he was, falling asleep when he had someone over.

He stood and stretched, then went to let Able out. He was stiff. Bad enough to fall asleep when Allie was over, but a night on the sofa hadn't done his body any good.

After a hot shower and fresh clothes, Jack felt better. He fed the dog and pulled out a heavy jacket to go out with Able for a quick walk, before heading for Portland. It was cold out, with a stiff breeze blowing in from the sea. He watched the white caps dance on the waves as they walked along the bluff. Able ran back and forth, the cast on his leg not hindering him at all. He barked at some birds, ran ahead and then back to sniff Jack, before taking off again.

They were both glad to get back inside the warm house. Allie would be arriving shortly and Jack didn't want to keep her waiting.

When her car turned into the drive, Jack felt a dart of

pure excitement. They'd spend the day together. Maybe he'd ask her for dinner again. He should have thought of that before. He couldn't keep ordering pizza. But it was too cold to grill steaks outside and he wasn't much of a cook otherwise.

"Good morning," she greeted him, when he opened the back door for Able and pulled down the ramp. "It's cold enough to snow if we were due any precipitation."

"We took a walk along the bluff. It's freezing," he said as he slid into the passenger seat.

"Hardy guys," she said.

"I didn't mean to fall asleep last night. Sorry about that."

"Hey, you were tired from the trip. Don't worry about it. I debated waking you up so you could go to bed, but you were really sound asleep."

"I used to be in much better shape," he mumbled, frustrated again at the new limitations he had to live with.

"I hope it's not this cold next week when we have the Veterans Day parade," she said. "We down-easterners are hardy, but many of the older folks like their creature comforts now and standing in the freezing wind isn't one of them!"

"Maybe no one will show up," he said

Allie laughed. "Don't count on that, soldier. There will still be plenty coming out to watch the parade."

Jack liked her laugh. He watched her as she drove, hoping he could say something else funny so she'd laugh again.

They ate lunch at a small café and left Able in the car. With the temperature dropping, it was cold enough he wouldn't be harmed. In fact, at one point Jack worried it was too cold to leave him in the car.

"We won't be that long. And he has a fur coat. I bet the cold didn't bother him at all this morning," Allie said.

"Not as much as it did me, that's for sure. He ran around like there was no problem with his leg, while mine aches more than ever in the cold."

The men greeted them warmly when they arrived at the community room. Sam came over to Jack.

"I hear I'm going home with you for a while. Right?"

"That's right. You ready today?"

"I guess. Can't remember anything else I have to do."

Jack smiled at his humor. "Maybe your memory will improve away from this place."

Sam looked at a card in his hand and nodded. "Dr. Murphy said to give it a few weeks. Then we reevaluate. And that I can go home with you today, if that works for you."

Jack saw he was reading from the card. He felt sorry for the guy. Head injuries were the worst. And they were so prevalent in this war. He might not walk like he used to, or hear, but at least his mind was sound. He wished there was something he could do for Sam's.

Sam looked over at Allie, already sitting and talking with a group of men. "Does she live there, too?"

"She lives in Rocky Point, but not in the house we'll be sharing."

"She's really pretty."

Jack turned to look at Allie, agreeing wholeheartedly with Sam. He took a deep breath. Today was the start of a new direction. He offered a brief prayer he'd be up to responsibilities. It was easy enough for Mason to say that Sam could get by almost on his own. It was the *almost* that worried Jack.

"Yeah, today works for me." He couldn't do anything else to prepare. In this, he was taking a page from Allie's book and trusting in God to have it come out right.

"Let me tell you about a parade we'll be in next week."

* * *

It was later than normal when the three of them reached Rocky Point that afternoon. Sam had his bag packed and was ready to leave, but the others at the facility took longer than expected telling him goodbye.

"Want to drive through town so Sam can see the place?" Allie asked.

"Good idea. You'll get a different perspective when we walk through, but we'll give you a glimpse now," Jack said, turning halfway around to see his new house mate.

Sam had been silent much of the ride, watching the scenery go by as if he'd never seen anything like it before.

Which he might not remember. Jack shook his head. This was going to be harder than he anticipated. What had Mason been thinking to suggest he be the one to help Sam?

"Thanks," Sam said.

Allie pointed out the different stores and shops as they slowly drove down the main street of town. Then she drove out Water Street to the end, pulling into Jack's driveway and stopping the car.

Jack looked at her. "Want to stay for dinner?"

"Sure."

It might help to have her around while he and Sam got situated. It wouldn't be just the two of them, but maybe that was better. He wouldn't fall asleep tonight.

And he would not get a chance to kiss her again, either.

* * *

Allie offered to make dinner after delivering the two men to the house at the end of Water Street. Because Jack had so little in the house, she also volunteered to make a run to the store. By the time she returned with all the ingredients for meatloaf and all the trimmings, Sam was settled in one of the upstairs bedrooms.

He and Jack were outside as Able ran around. Bundled against the cold, they seemed more than willing to brave the outdoors than remain inside.

"Aren't you guys freezing?" she asked, as they came to help with groceries.

"Once I get used to it, I'm fine. Beats sweltering in Afghanistan."

Sam decided to stay outside with Able, throwing the ball for him, laughing when the dog ran with his elevated leg.

Jack followed Allie into the kitchen.

"How's he doing?" she asked.

"Too early to tell. He has notes he refers to a lot. They help him keep track of things. I can't imagine waking up each morning and having to start over."

"Like that movie that was out years ago, where the guy kept repeating the same day."

"Only this isn't likely to change much. Though Mason said they are trying to reestablish patterns that will help him cope."

"So he can read."

"That part of the brain wasn't damaged as much as the part that holds memories. He can read. He's a whiz with numbers. He remembers colors and shapes. They think being in new surroundings and having to do more on his own will help. Or not. We're to take him back in a week when we go, have the doctors check on him."

Allie smiled, liking the sound of *we*. "Let me know what I can do to help," she said. "Think he'll like being in the Veteran's Day parade?"

"We'll find out. I thought I'd take him to meet George tomorrow. Be good for both of them. Plus I want to see how he's doing after our trip."

Allie could see the difference in the two men as they all ate dinner. Sam spoke little and was hesitant when he did. He asked her more than once what her name was, and didn't seem to be able to join in the conversation unless asked a direct question. Jack was easy going and compassionate with the other man. He had enough confidence for both of them, and she knew he'd do his best to help a fellow soldier.

Allie left as soon as the dishes had been done. It was the thing to do—to let them get established in a routine that would suit both of them. She could tell her presence confused Sam.

"I'll walk you out," Jack said, reaching for his jacket.

"It's cold out. I can manage," she said, as she pulled on her own coat.

"Able can go out with us," he said.

The night air was colder than she'd expected. She shivered, wishing her car would be warm, knowing the heater would likely not kick in much before she reached her place.

"Thanks for today. And for dinner. I think this is going to be harder than anyone thought," he said, as they walked to her car.

"Give him a few days. Change is hard on anyone, much more so for someone in Sam's predicament."

He stopped by her car and reached out to hold her shoulders. "I wish you'd stay a bit longer. I promise I won't fall asleep early tonight."

"No, I need to get home."

He stared at her in the darkness, barely visible with the light from the porch. Then he leaned closer and Allie knew he was going to kiss her again. She rose on tiptoes to meet him halfway and closed her eyes as his lips touched hers. It was magic. She stepped closer when his arms wrapped around her and put her own arms around him.

She loved Jack Donner.

She loved his kisses. She loved his courage. She loved his determination. She loved everything she knew about the man.

The thought rocked through her and caused her to pull back. Staring at Jack with wide eyes, she hoped her thoughts weren't readable.

"I have to go," she said and reached for the car door. She pulled away thirty seconds later, breathing hard, and in an absolute panic with her realization. She knew she liked the guy, but love? The kind that marriages were built on? When had that happened? What if he decided Rocky Point wasn't for him and he left? What if he stayed, but only saw her as a friend?

For the first time in a decade, Allie didn't want someone to see her as merely a friend. She wanted more. She wanted him to love her back.

* * *

Veteran's Day dawned bright and sunny. The temperature was rising and the forecast was for nice weather for the next several days. Allie was dressed and on her way to downtown before seven. She helped set up the flags that lined Main Street. Once that was done, she went to the table offering donuts and hot coffee, getting a cup to warm up with.

She went to her favorite spot that enabled her to get photos of all the participants--especially the car carrying the Grand Marshal. She hadn't seen Jack since last Thursday. She deliberately kept away, afraid of giving too much away. He knew where she was and if he wanted to see her, he could call her. He hadn't, and that bothered her. Maybe the feelings she experienced were all one-sided.

Still, she was looking forward to seeing him today, if only as he and George and Connor rode by in the car.

The sidewalks became crowded the closer to eleven

o'clock it became. The churches in town would begin the ringing of the bells at the eleventh hour. That signaled the start of the parade. As the time ticked down, more and more people arrived. Allie recognized many, and was constantly waving or calling hellos. Tom Daggart, the town's mayor, was standing in the small reviewing stand. He'd introduce each parade entry, telling funny stories, or explaining who was in the group. The loudspeakers had been set up all along Main Street.

Finally the bells began pealing. A cheer arose from the crowd and the high school band began playing the National Anthem as it started its march from the top of Main Street. Immediately behind them was the color guard from the National Guard unit. Everyone not already standing on the sidewalk stood, covering his or her heart as the American flag went by. Behind them came the convertible, carrying the Grand Marshals Jack, George and Connor. To Allie's amusement, Able sat in the passenger seat, a colorful red, white and blue bandanna around his neck. As people clapped, he barked his yelpy bark at the crowd, which brought laughter and more clapping.

Passing the reviewing stand, the men saluted the flag at the stand. Tom introduced them to the crowd. "Here are the heroes of Rocky Point," he said to a cheer. "These men put their lives on the line for all of us, to keep America the home of the free. Thank you, gentlemen, for your service!"

George beamed as the car slowly moved forward, waving at folks and calling names. Conner nodded and waved. Even Jack, looking fierce and strong, waved at the crowd. Each man wore his uniform and Allie caught her breath at how handsome Jack looked. She would never have met the man had he not been so severely injured in the war, but she was so sorry he couldn't do what he loved. She snapped a dozen pictures of them.

Please, Lord, she prayed silently, let him find a job that brings him joy.

Following the Grand Marshals were the local Veterans of Foreign Wars chapter. Then the Boy Scouts, the children's choir from Trinity Church singing patriotic songs, the DAR and SAR chapters. Group after group, some in floats, some walking, followed one another. Finally the equestrians marched by, the horses gleaming in the sunshine, their parade saddles dazzling with silver. The end of the parade had the traditional fire engine, which sounded its siren twice as it slowly moved down Main Street. Everyone clapped and cheered for each entry, and complained when the parade was over.

Just like every time, Allie thought, smiling. It was over until next year. She checked her camera. She had dozens of shots. She'd send them to the paper today, so they could run in the next issue.

Stores and shops along Main Street began opening for the remainder of the day. Business was always good on days when so many people came to town. Allie began walking down the sidewalk, stopping to talk to friends, greeting others in passing.

"Nice parade," a familiar voice said behind her.

She turned and smiled at Harriet. "It was. It always is, I think."

"I remember when you and Jason were in the children's choir. He was so proud when he marched in the parade."

"I remember all the hours we had to practice singing louder. Dottie Mansfield constantly drilled that into us." Allie smiled fondly at the happy memories from childhood.

Harriet nodded her expression one of sweet remembrance. "We still want you on the memorial committee. I understand now why you were championing that soldier. Susan told me there's another one living at the house now."

"Sam," Allie nodded, wondering what Harriet's rationale would be.

"You're always picking up strays, especially those wounded ones that need extra care. It's one of your endearing traits from when you were a little girl. I remember that hawk you rescued. Now you're rescuing injured soldiers. Such a do-gooder. Just like you rescued that dog. Once they get on their feet, I'm sure you'll move on to another cause. You can't save everyone, Allie."

"I'm not." Allie heard a sound behind her, and she turned to see Jack walking away.

* * *

Jack dodged two running kids and kept walking. His car was down by the park. He looked neither left nor right as he headed straight for it. *Rescuing injured soldiers* echoed in his mind. A do-gooder. He felt numb. *Just like you rescued that dog.* He refused to feel anything. Able trotted at his side. Turning his head, he barked and pulled on the leash. Jack jerked it once and the dog started walking beside him again. The crowd was dissipating, making it easier to increase his pace until he reached his car. Opening the back door, he half lifted Able into the car.

"Jack!"

He heard her, but refused to turn around. Getting into the car, he closed the door and started the engine. Looking behind him, it was safe to pull out. He drove directly to the house. Fool that he was he'd thought there was something special with Allie. Logic told him differently, but he thought they'd gone beyond logic. Who would want to tie herself to a man who couldn't do normal things, like shake hands?

Or hear when people spoke to him. Or a hundred different things that a whole man could do that he no longer could.

Allie rescued the injured. And was good at it. He glanced in the rearview mirror and saw Able's face. She'd rescued him. And forced the dog on him. Was that part of her plan: get the two injured critters to bond?

He refused to think about it. He had his way to make and, as of right now, he would do it without Miss Allie Turner!

He pulled into the driveway and sat, staring at the house. Sam was inside. He hadn't wanted to go to the parade. Jack couldn't desert the man. His first instinct was to regroup, retreat and start over somewhere else. But he had Sam to consider.

Where?

He shifted his glance and stared out at the sea. He liked

living here. He liked the quiet of the house, the walks he and Able took along the top of the rocky cliffs. He was getting stronger. He could do more now than when he first arrived.

And he was making friends.

At least he thought he had been. Were they all in on Allie's project? Time would tell.

He went inside.

"How did it go?" Sam asked from the sofa. He was reading a text book he'd brought from the VA. Beside him was the notebook he carried with notations to help him remember things.

"Lots of people, patriotic in a way I haven't seen before. It was good. You should have come."

"Maybe next year," Sam said.

Jack nodded. "I'm going to change." Next year. Would they both be here next year?

He couldn't think that far ahead. He was used to short term planning, strategizing the best way to defeat the enemy, not making long range plans on a life that was proving different than any he had ever imagined.

Once back in civvies, Jack headed downstairs. He needed a walk to clear his head. To get him thinking of the future. A future without Allie Turner in it. He didn't need some do-gooder holding his hand. He could make it on his own.

"I'm going for a walk, want to come?" he said to Sam.

"No, I'm still trying to figure this out. Take Able."

"Always," Jack said. He clicked his fingers and the dog leaped to his feet, tail wagging.

It was warmer than earlier in the week but not by much,

Jack thought as he and the dog walked along the edge of the cliff. The sea was a deep blue, dotted by whitecaps here and there. The breeze felt good after all, and he picked up the pace, his limp hardly noticeable. The dog ran ahead, then circled back, barking as if in pure joy. Jack laughed at Able's antics. "You are good to have around," he said.

He walked for an hour, returning home in a better frame of mind. Once inside, he headed for the kitchen. Past time to eat lunch.

Sam came into the kitchen, carrying his notebook.

"Did you eat?" Jack asked.

Sam nodded. "I think so. I have a message for you." He opened his book, read the notation and nodded again. "Allie came by. She wants you to call her. It's not what you think," Sam read carefully.

Jack hesitated a moment, then continued making his sandwich. "Thanks for the message," he said. He was not going to call her. Things were what they were; he'd learned that a long time ago.

The phone rang and he picked it up.

"Hey, Jack, Tate here. A bunch of us are going to Marcie's after lunch on Sunday and wanted to invite you and Sam. It'll be mostly the men's group from Bible study, but George said he'd join us. How about it? You two free?"

Jack almost refused, but he caught a glimpse of Sam studying his notebook and knew no matter how things had started, if they were to make a life in Rocky Point they had to join in the community. "We are. We'll meet you there after church." His heart pounded a bit with the decision, but he knew it was the right one.

"We've been invited to lunch after church on Sunday," he told Sam. "I accepted for us both."

"I won't know anyone," Sam said.

"I don't know many. We'll meet them together," Jack said.

"I don't know," Sam said, looking worried.

"Trust me. It'll work out."

* * *

Sunday morning, Allie arrived at church hoping she'd see Jack. She'd tried calling him twice since Veteran's Day, but both times the phone had just rung and rung. Didn't he have an answering machine? She'd left a message for him when she'd gone to his place after the parade. She knew Sam had written it down; had he remembered to tell Jack?

She hoped she'd see them both today. And have a chance to explain things to Jack.

When Bible study ended, she was caught by Melissa Downing, who wanted to talk about the Christmas pageant. Impatient to leave in hopes of catching Jack, Allie only gave her half her attention. "I can't decide this today. I'll get back to you," she finally said.

Hurrying to the foyer of the church, she stopped suddenly when she saw Jack and Sam enter.

"Jack, how are you?" Michelle hurried over to him and gave him a hug. He looked at her and smiled. He introduced Sam, while Allie just stood still. He'd come to church, but with Michelle holding his arm like she'd never let it go, Allie didn't know how she could explain anything to him. They needed a private moment. Or at least one where Michelle wasn't an audience.

The three of them entered the sanctuary without even noticing Allie.

She watched, and a moment later was bumped from behind.

"Sorry," Mrs. Dalvitch pushed passed, bumbling along as she talked to her friend Mrs. Cabot. The two older women entered the sanctuary. The organ had begun the prelude, and Allie took a deep breath. She'd have to catch Jack after the service.

Entering, she spotted Jack and Sam with Michelle only a few rows behind her parents. Hurrying up the aisle, she smiled at them as she passed. "Good morning," she said.

"Hi, Allie," Michelle responded.

Jack had his eyes on the bulletin in his hand. Sam looked over and nodded.

Unless she stood stock still until Jack raised his gaze, she had to move on. She slid into the pew beside her mother and resisted the urge to look behind her. Maybe he hadn't heard her.

Or maybe he had, and was ignoring her.

That hurt. She glanced at the bulletin, looking for anything so enthralling he couldn't raise his gaze long enough to greet her. There was nothing especially compelling.

When the singing began, Allie rose and joined in, darting one quick glance behind her. Her gaze clashed with Jack's.

He looked away, his face expressionless.

She frowned, trying to get into the hymn. It was unlike Jack to be deliberately rude. What was going on?

The sermon was a blur; all Allie could think about was getting a few minutes alone with Jack to find out what was wrong.

When the service ended, Allie was caught by several people who hadn't talked with her for a while, and by the time she reached the lawn of the church, Jack and Sam were long gone. No matter. She'd drive out to the house that afternoon after lunch with her parents.

The place was deserted when she arrived mid-afternoon. Jack's car was gone. Able wasn't around barking. Allie sat in the driveway for a long moment, wondering where he could be.

Giving up was not in her nature, but there was nothing to be done now. She'd try calling later.

* * *

Tuesday morning Allie finally reached Jack.

"I spoke to you Sunday in church, but I don't think you heard me."

"What can I do for you?" His voice sounded formal, distant.

"Actually, the vet called and wanted us to bring Able in for a check. He might be able to get the cast off." She was glad she had a strong reason to call, rather than acting like a lovesick teenager.

"When?"

"Today, if that works for you."

"It doesn't. I have plans. But you can take him in. The deal was I keep him until he could walk normally again and take the stairs at your place. He's already proved he can do that. I can drop him off and he'll be all yours."

"What? I thought you liked him."

"I do."

The silence went on for several moments.

"Okay, then. Bring him by before ten thirty, as his appointment is at eleven." Something definitely had changed in their relationship. Was it all from Harriet's damaging comment? Or was there more? From his tone, it didn't sound as if Jack wanted to resume the easy camaraderie they'd enjoyed.

She hadn't been imagining things. He had deliberately not spoken to her on Sunday. If that was the way of things, far be it from her to be clinging. She'd done just fine before Jack Donner showed up in Rocky Point, and she'd do just fine here on out.

Jack and Sam showed up at ten fifteen with Able. Before Allie could even get down the stairs, he had the dog's bed and a sack of toys and food unloaded from the car. Sam carried the bed up the stairs.

"Hi," he said with a smile.

She wasn't sure he remembered who she was. Obviously Jack had instructed him to carry up the bed.

He followed closely with the sack of food and toys, holding onto Able's leash. The little dog danced around him and wagged his tail when he saw Allie.

"Hi," she said.

"I have all his things here," he said.

She blocked the stairs and Jack came to a stop. His expression was stony. His eyes hard. For a moment, Allie wanted to reach out and sooth away the lines around his mouth. But when he held out the bag, she took it instinctively.

He looped the leash around her hand and leaned over to pet the dog. "Bye, Able. See you around."

Sam came back down. "I put the bed in the living room. I don't know where it goes."

"That's fine, man. Allie will decide where to put it. Come on, we don't want to be late."

Allie watched in disbelief as they got in Jack's car and drove way. Able barked after them, his tail still wagging.

"This is not how I pictured us going to the vet to get your cast off," Allie told Able when she drove to the vet's office in Pineville. She'd envisioned Jack and her celebrating when the little dog was free of the cast. Instead, he'd taken off, dumped the dog on her and left, as if he couldn't care less about Able. Allie thought they were perfect together. Obviously she'd missed some vital clue. How could he just leave his dog with her?

The visit lasted less than half hour. Allie drove through a drive-in fast food restaurant in Pineville for a quick lunch afterward. She didn't want to leave Able in the car alone, even though the weather was cool and a bit cloudy.

When they reached home, she kept tight hold on the leash so the dog wouldn't run away. Though it'd serve Jack right if Able did show up at his place. Didn't he realize the dog loved him?

Allie took Able with her to the VA Hospital on Thursday. She didn't call Jack to see if he wanted to go. He'd made it pretty clear that he didn't want anything to do with her and she was not going to go where not wanted. The men were glad to see her and Able, and the afternoon passed swiftly. She felt a little sad that Jack hadn't come—especially when some of the men asked after him and showed their own disappointment that he hadn't accompanied her today.

She missed him herself. The ride home seemed endless. No one to talk to about what had gone on. No one to share the amazing recovery of Josh, or laugh at the antics some of the men had got up to with Able. She sighed. He'd only gone with her a few times. How could she miss him so much?

The few weeks he'd lived in Rocky Point had changed her life forever. She'd fallen in love and would never been the same.

"So, Lord, let me know what to do now, please," she prayed aloud, as she reached the outskirts of town. "If it is to be, show me the way. If not, help me find understanding and compassion and to be happy if his life is happy."

When she reached home, Able hopped out of the car and raced up the steps. She laughed. "Okay, is it dinner time already?"

He barked. She started up the steps and he raced by her, heading for the road.

"No! Able, come! Come back here." She turned on the stairs and watched as he sped down the road toward town, and Water Street and the house where Jack lived.

Allie debated following the dog. Maybe if he showed up, Jack would realize how much he'd missed Able and want to keep him.

Or maybe the man wasn't even home. Sighing, she walked back to the car and headed for Jack's house. She had said she'd keep the dog once he was well. She just hadn't expected Jack to give him up.

When she reached Jack's house, Allie saw Michelle's car in the drive behind Jack's. Able was already on the porch, barking at the front door. When it opened, Allie saw Sam's look of surprise. He looked at her as she got out of the car.

"Hi," he said.

"Hi, Sam. Is Jack around?"

"No, he went for a walk."

Michelle came to the dog and smiled at Allie. "He headed that way." She pointed beyond the house where the cliff curved around. "I'm helping Sam with some memory techniques. Jack said he wanted the exercise. I hope you're dressed warmly; the wind is freezing."

It was cooler than at her house, but Allie was a downeasterner from the get-go. It felt invigorating.

She started walking in the direction Michelle indicated. Her hip ached a little, but she ignored it, wondering how far Jack had gone. She couldn't see him. Able raced past her and continued full speed. In the distance, she saw Jack. Able would reach him in moments. It would take her a while. But she kept walking.

She saw the dog reach Jack. In only a moment, both of

them headed back toward her. At least the distance would be cut if he met her part way.

* * *

Jack recognized the dog's bark immediately and turned to see Able racing toward him. He smiled. He'd missed that dog. Not that he'd let Allie know. Looking beyond the streaking brown and white ball of fur, he could see Allie walking his way. Able danced around him in frantic greeting, shaking all over in delight.

"Hey, boy, how're you doing? What are you two doing here? Come to take care of the invalid again?" He rubbed the dog's body, noticing the lack of cast.

"So you're all fit again. With no limp, I see. Better than I turned out. Come on, let's head back. You need to go with Allie."

Had she come for some reason? He'd been thinking about her for days. Wishing he could change things. Wishing he didn't know why she'd spent so much time with him, to go back to when he thought they had something developing between them. Which was plain stupid. He could never get involved with her. She'd done her bit; the rest of his life was up to him.

Still, he couldn't help noticing how pretty she looked as they walked closer to each other. The cold wind brought color to her cheeks. Her eyes sparkled and her hair whipped around in the breeze. He knew her hip had to be bothering her, but he couldn't tell from the look of happiness on her face. Which changed to caution the closer they got.

"Hi," she said, when he was close enough to hear her.

"What are you doing out here?" he asked, more sharply than he wanted. But seeing her hurt his heart.

"Your dog left my home and came back to you. This is what happened when you took George to Washington. He's okay to visit me, but he belongs to you. Just look at him."

Able hadn't left Jack's side since he'd caught up with him. He looked at Jack with adoration, his tail wagging furiously.

"The deal--" Jack started to say, but Allie interrupted.

"Able didn't make any deal. He doesn't understand. He's yours. I can take him home every day, but my guess is he'll find ways to escape and head back to you. What's wrong with keeping him?"

"That's your thing, not mine. I don't need to take in every stray that comes along. He's healed now and if you want to keep him, fine. If not--" Jack looked at the dog sitting at his side, his gaze never leaving Jack's face.

"What do you mean it's my thing? You wouldn't have stopped to help if you'd seen him?"

Jack shrugged. He wouldn't have left a dog to suffer on the side of the road. But a man was different from a dog. He didn't need saving. He would find his way doing whatever it took.

"Save a dog. Save a soldier. Isn't that what you do? Harriet Lodge said it--you're always picking up strays. So Sam and I qualified, but now we can make it on our own. We don't need you anymore."

The stricken look on her face pierced him. He wanted to

stay away but that expression broke his heart. He didn't need to be so scathing about things.

"I appreciate all you've done for me," he began.

She held up a hand. "Stop. Don't say another word." Turning, Allie began walking back toward the house and her car.

Jack stared after her. He was still seething over the idea of her taking him on as a stray, like the dog. He'd thought they were friends. He enjoyed her company—too much actually. Once in the middle of a sleepless night, he'd even fantasized a little about getting some job that would enable him to support a wife—and Allie had been the woman he'd wanted.

He still wanted her.

Her head held high, she walked steadily away. He felt as if something special had died. Maybe it had. His hope for a future with a pretty woman, who understood more than anyone.

A woman who had never married. Who would be terrific with kids. Who would encourage children to bring home strays and help them get better. And turn them loose.

She hadn't turned him loose.

"Allie," he called, starting after her.

She continued walking.

"Allie, wait."

As if she hadn't heard him, she walked ahead. She wasn't halfway deaf, she had to hear him.

"Did I get it wrong?" he asked, a tiny ray of hope in his tone. What if he'd gotten it wrong and she did care? She was the best thing that had ever happened to him, and he'd just hurt her and virtually told her he didn't want anything to do with her.

He used to be able to run twenty miles in full gear. He was lucky to walk a couple of miles with a limp that was gradually improving these days. He began to run. Able ran beside him, barking at the new game.

Jack reached Allie and caught her arm in his hand, pulling her to a stop. Shocked to see tears streaking down her cheeks, he gave a groan and pulled her into his arms, cradling her head against his chest.

"I'm sorry," he said. "I'm so sorry. I didn't mean to make you cry. Please, Allie. Hear me out."

"What's left to say. Haven't you made yourself clear?"

"I'm not sure what I'm saying. Did you befriend me just to help an injured soldier out? Take me on as a project as Harriet said?"

She shook her head.

"Then what?"

"Never mind."

"Tell me."

She was silent so long, he thought she wouldn't reply, then her voice came, muffled against his jacket.

"Because you were special from the get-go."

He almost reeled back. No one had ever said he was special.

"Harriet said you were always taking on strays. I thought that's why you helped me," he explained.

She said something, but he couldn't hear it.

"What?" He reached under her chin and tilted her face up to see her.

"Harriet is trying to find a reason for me to be the woman she wants me to be--totally focused on Jason. I think my interest in another man really shook her."

"Interest, huh?"

She nodded, her eyes holding his.

"How interested?" he asked.

"Lots."

He wasn't sure what that meant. "So what is lots?"

"Does it matter? You don't want to even talk to me."

"We're talking now, aren't we? I'm interested in you, too, you know."

"How interested?"

He laughed. She was turning his words back on him. The truth stared him in the face. Was he brave enough to voice it? He had done his duty in the Army, faced the enemy with all the courage he could muster. Could he do this?

"Enough to say I love you, Allie Turner."

She blinked and a dazzling smile illuminated her face.

"You do? Jack, I love you!"

Only one thing to do with a statement like that, he kissed her. She kissed him back and flung her arms around him, her cane dropping to the ground.

Several minutes later he broke the kiss, resting his forehead against hers. "I don't have a job. Don't even have very many prospects of getting a good-paying job. I can't hear well, can't walk without a limp and don't know if my arm will ever regain enough mobility to be worthwhile. But I want you, Allie. I love everything I know about you. I don't know what kind of future I'll have, but when I get there, I want you with me."

"When you get there?"

"I need to find a job that will support a wife and family. I thought I'd never have one. You changed that. One day--"

"Step out in faith, Jack. Let's make that day soon."

He hesitated. Things were spinning out of control. Or were they? Hadn't her faith brought him back to the Lord? Didn't he believe now that God did have a plan for him? He was still feeling his way, but his faith grew stronger every day. Step out in faith, she'd said. He could do that.

"Will you marry me?" Jack asked, looking deep into her eyes. He saw only love and happiness.

"Yes! Oh, Jack, I love you so much. I've waited for years to find someone special to love. Let's not wait too long before we set a date to begin our lives together."

"I need--"

Allie put her fingers on his lips. "Shhh. We can step out in faith, knowing the Lord will take care of things. He brought us together, I'm convinced of that. Where else would I find a man who understood about my own injuries?"

"Who isn't whole and won't ever be."

"Me, either. But together, we can do wondrous things."

"I want that strong faith you have. To know I can trust God to lead us and make things happen for us. I've already come back to more physical abilities than I thought I would five months ago. There's still so much more to do. I know now the Lord has a plan for me. I think it's going to be helping with other veterans. Not sure of all the ins and outs, but I want to help where I can. I need the Lord to lead me."

"He will. He has. I believe in miracles and you are my miracle. You weren't killed in that attack. You came to live here, you love me. I find that all amazing."

"You're the reason I came to Rocky Point. I loved the stories you told at the VA. I wanted to find that kind of home for myself, those kinds of friends. Your kind of faith."

"We'll make a home full of love. We already have loads of friends here in town. You'll always belong here. If there are doubts, let's blow them away. I'm who I am, and you are who you are and I wouldn't change a single thing right now even if I could. I love you, Jack. I believe you're the man God sent to complete my life."

He gazed into her pretty eyes, feeling the love almost overwhelm him. This beautiful woman loved him just the way he was. Allie was his miracle. Jack kissed her again. There were many aspects to discuss. He wasn't as sure as she was that an early marriage date was what they should do. But now that she'd said yes, he couldn't wait to make her his wife and begin that stage of their lives.

He would look to the Lord to provide the way. He would be content with whatever came, as long as Allie was by his side. And if the Lord blessed them with children, he would be happier than he ever expected.

Once he thought the Army would be his life forever. Now he knew it had been a stepping stone to his coming here.

Thank you, Lord, for this miracle. Allie was right—it was amazing.

Able barked, as if in total agreement.

—The End—

Did you enjoy this story? If so you may enjoy *Rocky Point Box Set Books 1-3* or *Rocky Point Inn*

More books by Barbara McMahon

The Harts of Texas Series
Rebel Heart
Tangled Hearts
Reckless Heart

Cowboy Heroes Series
Blue Bells on the Hill
Cowboy's Bride
One Stubborn Cowboy
Crazy About a Cowboy
Never Doubt a Cowboy
Cowboy Marshal
Summer Cowboy
Second Chance Cowboy
Movie Star Cowboy

Tropical Escape Series
Island Rendezvous
Come into the Sun
Island Paradise
Destination Romance Boxed Set

Elite Security Mystery Series
Trusting Jake

Rocky Point Series
Rocky Point Legacy
Rocky Point Reunion
Rocky Point Promise
Rocky Point Hero
Rocky Point Inn

The Ultimate Billionaires
The Cynical Sheikh
Falling for the Sheikh
A Sheikh of Her Own
The Unforgettable Sheikh

Other Books
A Soldier's Christmas
I'll Take Forever
Jared's Promise
The Paper Marriage
The Christmas Locket
The Banished Bride
Cowboy Charade
The Cowboy's Special Christmas
Mail Order Bride
Because of You
Sweet Meant To Be